EIGHT
STORIES

THE NEW DIRECTIONS *Bibelots*

DYLAN THOMAS

EIGHT STORIES

A NEW DIRECTIONS

Bibelot

These eight stories are selections from *The Collected Stories* of Dylan
Thomas (New Directions, 1984).

Manufactured in the United States of America
New Directions Books are printed on acid-free paper.
First published as a New Directions Bibelot in 1993
Published simultaneously in Canada by Penguin Books Canada
Limited

Library of Congress Cataloging in Publication Data

Thomas, Dylan, 1914-1953.
    [Short Stories. Selections]
    Eight stories / Dylan Thomas.
        p.   cm.   "A New Directions bibelot."
    "These eight stories are selections from The collected stories
    of Dylan Thomas, New Directions, 1984"—CIP galley.
    ISBN 0-8112-1245-9
    1. Wales—Fiction.   I. Title.   II. Title: 8 stories.
PR6039.H52A6   1993   823'.912—dc20   93-409   CIP

New Directions Books are published for James Laughlin
by New Directions Publishing Corporation,
80 Eighth Avenue, New York 10011

FOURTH PRINTING

The End of the River

Twelve generations of the Quincey family, that dogfaced line, had left their mark upon the manor. The walls remained steadfast, but covered with a green fungus that sprouted upon the Quincey habitations, regardless of pruning. The gardener had not neglected the lawns, and the flower-beds, though pale and blowsy, were tended with all his senile care, for Chubb could never die, bound, as he was, so inextricably to the Quincey bosom. But weeds grew thick where weeds were little expected to grow. Ivy climbed up the walls of the coach house, and, in spite of the daily attentions of the youngest housemaid but one, moss invaded the front steps and rust lay thick upon the knocker. Hens upon the bird-limed patch beyond the kitchen died at a premature age, while the eggs they contrived to lay were rarely oval and often of a withered shape and a rather unpleasant mottled colour. The pigs were fed as heartily as pigs could wish, but they grew thin and died. The cows' milk tasted like vinegar.

The Quincey manor, with its portrait gallery of canine gentlemen, its dining-hall furnished in three periods, and its perilous verandahs from which the bloodless Quinceys, on midsummer nights, would pass their gravish comments on the moon, had resolved to crumble, spurning renovations and improvements, sitting on the camel hill over the disagreeable river, waiting for its end.

And Sir Peregrine, twelfth baron, had nothing but sympathy for it. It had sheltered twelve generations of doggy aristocrats and their litters, had seen small boys grow to be small men, had seen them meet, mate, and lie, at last, in the depths of the family vault, their dead paws on their chests. It had entertained near-royalty, and consequently had allotted a royal bedroom to its left wing. Over all the passions of a most impure world it had spread its painted roofs, and, on one notable occasion, had hidden, in a cellar full of stale wine and rats, the murdered body of poor Sir Thomas.

The manor, thought Sir Peregrine, was old enough to die, had pondered enough upon the human follies and felt no fear of death.

Stroking a three-days' beard, he placed a deck-chair on the safest part of the verandah, looked up into the sun and turned to the year 1889 in the Quincey Chronicles.

Somewhere a romantic daughter spelt out her Sunday music. His lady, in the quiet of her room, was writing to an Australian cousin. In his apartment the butler was reading from the literary pages of the *Observer*. Chubb, in the not very far distance, leaned on a garden gate and smoked.

Peregrine, read the twelfth baron from the Chronicles, took up the title on the death of his father, Belphigor, in 1889. In 1902 he married the Honourable Katerina Hautley, second daughter of Lord and Lady Winch of Alltheway Park, Gloucestershire. From this union were born three daughters: Katerina, who died of influenza in her second year, Astasia, and Phoebe Mary. Sir Peregrine was a colonel in the Territorial Army up to the Great War (1914-1918), and an official in the Ministry of War during those troubled years. He was elected Master of the Tidhampton Hunt in 1920, following upon the death of Alderman Alcock, and in 1922 broke his arm while riding with the hounds. In the following year Phoebe Mary married the Honourable Douglas Dougal, son of Sir Douglas and Lady Dougal of Halfandhalf Castle, Perth. In 1924 Phoebe Mary died in childbirth.

That was all. The Chronicles of the previous Quincey generations were written in detail and with an ornamentation of style that did credit to the literary accomplishments of the family. But Sir Peregrine dealt in facts, and facts alone. His life until that moment, but shorn of its hopes and foolishness, its strength and weaknesses, delights and dolours, spread over half a page of the ponderous book. This little life set between the eccentricities of the longwinded Belphigor and...

Sir Peregrine put the book down.

Chubb was still leaning and smoking. The smoke rose up vertically into the windless air. Chubb had not moved. His eyes rested on the river which went Sir Peregrine knew not where, meandering, he supposed, through a world of fields and rushes, making noise over pebbles, till it came to a sudden stop. He had always called it the one river that did not wind safely to the sea.

Astasia had stopped her playing.

Life was good, he found, on most Sunday afternoons. But to-day he was restless, and could not sit, as he had for so many years, dreamily upon the verandah, feeling the world grow and hum around him, hearing the music of a sweetly untuned piano or the songs of birds.

The day was beautiful. Clouds sailed on the sky. There was a warm sun. He looked down to where the Chronicles lay at his feet, and knew, quite suddenly and almost happily, all that was the matter. The time had come for the dissolution of the Quinceys, for the fall of their manor and the end of their dynasty.

Sir Peregrine, lifting the book, took out a pencil used to a stump through the solving of innumerable crossword puzzles.

In 1924 he read again, Phoebe Mary died in childbirth.

Phoebe Mary had been his favourite daughter. He had cried for six nights after she was buried. Then he, too, had buried her, under the clouds and mists of his mind. Once he had forgotten her name. Phoebe Mary? he said, and had fallen to wondering who that could be with such a name.

Phoebe Mary died in childbirth.

The end of the Quinceys, he wrote with the pencil.

Then he added the date.

In the garden he looked around him, at the flowers whose colours were as even as those in a toy paint box. The little wind there was moved the petals so that they seemed, to him, to breathe for the last time the sweet air of the surrounding beds. He knew they were aware of climax, and loved them for their serenity. Chubb had nurtured them, and the end of the world would see the gardener like a god, waiting in a woman's blue smock, for his reward.

The end of the world was the end of the manor. And Chubb, though he would say nothing of it, neither affirm nor contradict, had tended the first bed for the first young baron.

Sir Peregrine found him at the end of the path. The gardener did not move. His arms were resting on the gate that led to the seven fields going down to the river.

Sir Peregrine, wiping a remnant of dinner from his ancient waistcoat, looked down to where the water rolled over the dirty stones. At the end of the water was the end of everything. Today he was to walk over the fields and follow the river where it went, through towns or countries, over hills or under, until the sudden stop.

The garden was humming behind them.

The clouds moved on softly to some stop.

How old are you, Chubb? asked Sir Peregrine. You were the

gardener here when Lady Astasia rode to her Queen, Elizabeth, over the rocky roads on a piebald horse. You tended the flowers when Quentin, third of the Quinceys, wrote to his lady in an ivory tower, wrapping the verses round a pigeon's throat. At Christmas you made snowmen for me. How many years have you brooded over the dirty river? You always knew the end of all things lay where it stopped. I only knew to-day. It came to me suddenly and I knew.

The immortal Chubb made no answer. He tilted his felt hat further back on his head, and sent up a ring of smoke from a white pipe. His face, fringed with a yellowing beard, was as round and expressionless as a saucer. At any time a breath of wind might send another crack along its surface, and make a thousand smiles or frowns. Through a space in his teeth he breathed and whistled, and made a succession of mysterious tunes as he drew at his pipe.

The exterior Chubb belied what was divine beneath. He looked like nothing more than an ancient gardener, with his woman's smock pinned untidily around him.

Chubb, I am going.

Sir Peregrine waited for the words to pierce the gardener's smoky armour.

I am going to follow the river to its end. Tell me one word of cheer before I go. Say good-bye, undying Chubb.

The birds, said the gardener, 'ave 'ad the seeds.

It was enough. Sir Peregrine climbed quickly over the gate and ran down the field. At the end was a stile. He climbed it, and ran again over the uneven grass, his hair leaping about his head and his brass-buttoned waistcoat flapping against his sides. Three fields. Four fields. Sweat ran down his forehead on to his neck and collar. He could hear his heart thundering in his ears. But he kept at the same crazy jog, over another stile, along another field, stopping to climb through a small hole in the hedge, then on again, snorting and blowing.

A crow, perched on a scarecrow's shoulder, suddenly started cawing as the twelfth baron galloped past, then flew above him, spurring him on with harsh cries.

Now he could hear the noise of the river. On the low bank above it, he stared down on to the little fishes and the shining pebbles. The crow, seeing him stop, gave a final sardonic caw, and flew back to its lone companion, who was swinging a ragged arm in the wind.

Sir Peregrine felt a great elation surging through him. He turned around, and saw the Quincey manor, on its imperial hill, squinting down upon him. He followed the river bank through the dirty fields and through a wood brown with owls' wings. He saw the sun lowering in the sky. Now he no longer ran, but stumbled over the fields, his eyes dim, covered in tears, half unseeing. His clothes were damp about him. His hair that had, in the mad run down the seven fields, leapt so proudly on his head, straggled on to his wet brow. He was thirsty and tired. But he stumbled on.

Where does the river end? he called out to an old woman driving cows over a green field.

Where does it end? he asked. But the hedges and the ferns and the talking pebbles never replied.

He came at last to a well by the side of a meadow, and there a girl-child was washing clothes. He saw her through his tears and heard her voice singing.

Is this the end?

Yes, said the girl-child.

The end, said Sir Peregrine in a whisper. The end of the manor, the Quinceys, and me.

The words made such a nice little rhythm that he started to sing them in his old voice.

The end of the manor, the Quinceys and me.

The child was frightened.

For twelve generations, he said, the Quinceys have lived their little lives up there. And he pointed with a bewildered hand towards the sky. This is the end, he said.

Yes, said the child.

What is the end? he said. What have you to give? What at the end?

He held his arms out.

With a frightened cry, the girl-child thrust an un-washed napkin into his hand. He clasped it, and she ran away. Not looking, but holding it to his breast and making soft, delighted noises in his throat, Sir Peregrine lay down upon the grass. The moon came up. Chubb had not failed.

And that immortal gardener, as the twelfth baron lay down on a bed of grass and soft manure, was smoking a white pipe in the quiet of the Quincey gardens. Sunday was almost passed, and then there would be another day. Contentedly the ancient gardener, in his woman's smock, leaned on the garden gate and smoked.

The School for Witches

On Cader Peak there was a school for witches where the doctor's daughter, teaching the unholy cradle and the devil's pin, had seven country girls. On Cader Peak, half ruined in an enemy weather, the house with a story held the seven girls, the cellar echoing, and a cross reversed above the entrance to the inner rooms. Here the doctor, dreaming of illness, in the centre of the tubercular hill, heard his daughter cry to the power swarming under the West roots. She invoked a particular devil, but the gehenna did not yawn under the hill, and the day and the night continued with their two departures; the cocks crew and the corn fell in the villages and yellow fields as she taught the seven girls how the lust of man, like a dead horse, stood up to his injected mixtures. She was short and fat-thighed; her cheeks were red; she had red lips and innocent eyes. But her body grew hard as she called to the black flowers under the tide of roots; when she fetched the curdlers out of the trees to bore through the cows' udders, the seven staring stared at the veins hardening in her breast; she stood uncovered, calling the devil, and the seven uncovered closed round her in a ring.

Teaching them the intricate devil, she raised her arms to let him enter. Three years and a day had vanished since she first bowed to the moon, and, maddened by the mid light, dipped her hair seven times in the salt sea, and a mouse in honey. She stood, still untaken, loving the lost man; her fingers hardened on light as on the breastbone of the unentering devil.

Mrs. Price climbed up the hill, and the seven saw her. It was the first evening of the new year, the wind was motionless on Cader Peak, and a half red, promising dusk floated over the rocks. Behind the midwife the sun sank as a stone sinks in a marsh, the dark bubbled over it, and the mud sucked it down into the bubble of the bottomless fields.

In Bethlehem there is a prison for mad women, and in Cathmarw by the parsonage trees a black girl screamed as she laboured. She was afraid to die like a cow on the straw, and to the noises of the rooks. She screamed for the doctor on Cader Peak as the tumultuous West moved in its grave. The midwife heard her.

A black girl rocked in her bed. Her eyes were stones. Mrs. Price climbed up the hill, and the seven saw her.

Midwife, midwife, called the seven girls. Mrs. Price crossed herself. A chain of garlic hung at her throat. Carefully, she touched it. The seven cried aloud, and ran from the window to the inner rooms where the doctor's daughter, bent on uncovered knees, counselled the black toad, her familiar, and the divining cat slept by the wall. The familiar moved its head. The seven danced, rubbing the white wall with their thighs until the blood striped the thin symbols of fertility upon them. Hand in hand they danced among dark symbols, under the charts that marked the rise and fall of the satanic seasons, and their white dresses swung around them. The owls commenced to sing, striking against the music of the suddenly awaking winter. Hand in hand the dancers spun around the black toad and the doctor's daughter, seven stags dancing, their antlers shaking, in the confusion of the unholy room.

She is a very black woman, said Mrs. Price, and curtsied to the doctor.

He woke to the midwife's story out of a dream of illness, remembering the broken quicked, the black patch and echo, the mutilated shadows of the seventh sense.

She lay with a black scissor-man.

He wounded her deep, said the doctor, and wiped a lancet on his sleeve.

Together they stumbled down the rocky hill.

A terror met them at the foot, the terror of the blind tapping their white sticks and the stumps of the arms on the solid darkness; two worms in the foil of a tree, bellies on the rubber sap and the glues of a wrong-grained forest, they, holding tight to hats and bags, crawled now up the path that led to the black birth. From right, from left, the cries of labour came in under the branches, piercing the dead wood, from the earth where a mole sneezed, and from the sky, out of the worms' sight.

They were not the only ones caught that night in the torrential blindness; to them, as they stumbled, the land was empty of men, and the prophets of bad weather alone walked in their neighbourhoods. Three tinkers appeared out of silence by the chapel wall. Capel Cader, said the panman. Parson is down on tinkers, said John Bucket. Cader Peak, said the scissor-man, and up they went. They passed the midwife close; she heard the scissors clacking, and the branch of a tree drum on the buckets. One, two, three, they were gone, invisibly shuffling as she hugged her skirts. Mrs. Price crossed herself for the second time that day, and touched the garlic at her throat. A vampire with a scissors was a Pembroke devil. And the black girl screamed like a pig.

Sister, raise your right hand. The seventh girl raised her right hand. Now say, said the doctor's daughter, Rise up out of the bearded barley. Rise out of the green grass asleep in Mr. Griffith's dingle. Big man, black man, all eye, one tooth, rise up out of Cader marshes. Say the devil kisses me. The devil kisses me, said the girl cold in the centre of the kitchen. Kiss me out of the bearded barley. Kiss me out of the bearded barley. The girls giggled in a circle. Swive me out of the green grass. Swive me out of the green grass. Can I put on my clothes now? said the young witch, after encountering the invisible evil.

Throughout the hours of the early night, in the smoke of the seven candles, the doctor's daughter spoke of the sacrament of darkness. In her familiar's eyes she read the news of a great and an unholy coming; divining the future in the green and sleepy eyes, she saw, as clearly as the tinkers saw the spire, the towering coming of a beast in stag's skin, the antlered animal whose name read backwards, and the black, black, black wanderer climbing a hill for the seven wise girls of Cader. She woke the cat. Poor Bell, she said, smoothing his fur the wrong way. And, Ding dong, Bell, she said, and swung the spitting cat.

Sister, raise your left hand. The first girl raised her left hand. Now with your right hand put a needle in your left hand. Where is a needle? Here, said the doctor's daughter, Is a needle, here in your hair. She made a gesture over the black hair, and drew a needle out from the coil at her ear. Say I cross you. I cross you, said the girl, and, with the needle in her hand, struck at the black cat racked on the daughter's lap.

For love takes many shapes, cat, dog, pig, or goat; there was a lover, spellbound in the time of mass, now formed and featured in the image of the darting cat; his belly bleeding, he sped past the seven girls, past parlour and dispensary, into the night, on to the hill; the wind got at his wound, and swiftly he darted down the rocks, in the direction of the cooling streams.

He passed the three tinkers like lightning. Black cat is luck, said the panman. Bloody cat is bad luck, said John Bucket. The scissorman said nothing. They appeared out of silence by the wall of the Peak house, and heard a hellish music through the open door. They peered through the stained-glass window, and the seven girls danced before them. They have beaks, said the panman. Web feet, said John Bucket. The tinkers walked in.

At midnight the black girl bore her baby, a black beast with the eyes of a kitten and a stain at the corner of its mouth. The midwife, remembering birthmarks, whispered to the doctor of the gooseberry on his daughter's arm. Is it ripe yet? said Mrs. Price. The doctor's hand trembled, and his lancet cut the baby under the chin. Scream you, said Mrs. Price, who loved all babies.

The wind howled over Cader, waking the sleepy rooks who cawed from the trees and, louder than owls, disturbed the midwife's meditations. It was wrong for the rooks, those sleepy birds over the zinc roofs, to caw at night. Who put a spell on the rooks? The sun might rise at ten past one in the morning.

Scream you, said Mrs. Price, the baby in her arms, This is a wicked world. The wicked world, with a voice out of the wind, spoke to the baby half smothering under the folds of the midwife's overcoat. Mrs. Price wore a man's cap, and her great breasts heaved under the black blouse. Scream you, said the wicked world, I am an old man blinding you, a wicked little woman tickling you, a dry death parching you. The baby screamed, as though a flea were on its tongue.

The tinkers were lost in the house, and could not find the inner room where the girls still danced with the beaks of birds upon them and their web feet bare on the cobblestones. The panman opened the dispensary door, but the bottles and the tray of knives alarmed him. The passages were too dark for John Bucket, and the scissorman surprised him at a corner. Christ defend me, he cried. The girls stopped dancing, for the name of Christ rang in the outer halls. Enter, and, Enter, cried the doctor's daughter to the welcome devil. It was the scissorman who found the door and turned the handle, walking into candlelight. He stood before Gladwys on the threshold, a giant black as ink with a three days' beard. She lifted her face to his, and her sackcloth fell away.

Up the hill, the midwife, cooing as she came, held the newborn baby in her arms, and the doctor toiled behind her with his black bag rattling. The birds of the night flew by them, but the night was empty, and these restless wings and voices, hindering emptiness forever, were the feathers of shadows and the accents of an invisible flying. What purpose there was in the shape of Cader

Peak, in the bouldered breast of the hill and the craters poxing the green-black flesh, was no more than the wind's purpose that willy nilly blew from all corners the odd turfs and stones of an unmoulded world. The grassy rags and bones of the steep hill were, so the doctor pondered as he climbed behind the baby rocking into memory on a strange breast, whirled together out of the bins of chaos by a winter wind. But the doctor's conceits came to nothing, for the black child let out a scream so high and loud that Mr. Griffiths heard it in his temple in the dingle. The worshipper of vegetables, standing beneath his holy marrow nailed in four places to the wall, heard the cry come down from the heights. A mandrake cried on Cader. Mr. Griffiths hastened in the direction of the stars.

John Bucket and the panman stepped into candlelight, seeing a strange company. Now in the centre circle of the room, surrounded by the unsteady lights, stood the scissorman and a naked girl; she smiled at him, he smiled at her, his hands groped for her body, she stiffened and slackened, he drew her close, smiling she stiffened again, and he licked his lips.

John Bucket had not seen him as a power for evil baring the breasts and the immaculate thighs of the gentlewomen, a magnetic blackman with the doom of women in his smile, forcing open the gates of love. He remembered a black companion on the roads, sharpening the village scissors, and, in the shadows, when the tinkers took the night, a coal-black shadow, silent as the travelling hedges.

Was this tall man, the panman murmured, who takes the doctor's daughter with no how-d'you-do, was he Tom the scissorman? I remember him on the highways in the heat of the sun, a black, three-coated tinker.

And, like a god, the scissorman bent over Gladwys, he healed her wound, she stood his ointment and his fire, she burned at the tower altar, and the black sacrifice was done. Stepping out of his arms, her offering cut and broken, the gut of a lamb, she smiled and cried manfully: Dance, dance, my seven. And the seven danced, their antlers shaking, in the confusion of the unholy room. A coven, a coven, cried the seven as they danced. They beckoned the panman from the door. He edged towards them, and they caught his hands. Dance, dance, my strange man, the seven cried. John Bucket joined them, his buckets drumming, and swiftly they dragged him into the rising fury of the dance. The scissorman in the circle danced like a tower. They sped round and round, none crying louder than the two tinkers in the heart of the swirling company, and lightly the doctor's daughter was among them. She drove them to a faster turn of foot; giddy as weathercocks in a hundred changing winds, they were revolving figures in the winds of their dresses and to the music of the scissors and the metal pans; giddily she spun between the dancing hoops, the wheels of cloth and hair, and the bloody ninepins spinning; the candles grew pale and lean in the wind of the dance; she whirled by the tinker's side, by the scissorman's side, by his dark, damp side, smelling his skin, smelling the seven furies.

It was then that the doctor, the midwife, and the baby entered through the open door as quietly as could be. Sleep well, Pembroke, for your devils have left you. And woe on Cader Peak that the black man dances in my house. There had been nothing for that savage evening but an end of evil. The grave had yawned, and the black breath risen up.

Here danced the metamorphoses of the dusts of Cathmarw. Lie level, the ashes of man, for the phoenix flies from you, woe unto Cader, into my nice, square house. Mrs. Price fingered her garlic, and the doctor stood grieving.

The seven saw them. A coven, a coven, they cried. One, dancing past them, snatched at the doctor's hand; another, dancing caught him around the waist; and, all bewildered by the white flesh of their arms, the doctor danced. Woe, woe on Cader, he cried as he swirled among maidens, and his steps gathered speed. He heard his voice rising; his feet skimmed over the silver cobbles. A coven, a coven, cried the dancing doctor, and bowed in his measures.

Suddenly Mrs. Price, hugging the black baby, was surrounded at the entrance of the room. Twelve dancers hemmed her in, and the hands of strangers pulled at the baby on her breast. See, see, said the doctor's daugher, The cross on the black throat. There was blood beneath the baby's chin where a sharp knife had slipped and cut. The cat, cried the seven, The cat, the black cat. They had unloosed the spellbound devil that dwelt in the cat's shape, the human skeleton, the flesh and heart out of the gehenna of the valley roots and the image of the creature calming his wound in the far-off streams. Their magic was done; they set the baby down on the stones, and the dance continued. Pembroke, sleep well, whispered the dancing midwife, Lie still, you empty county.

And it was thus that the last visitor that night found the thirteen dancers in the inner rooms of Cader House: a black man and a blushing girl, two shabby tinkers, a doctor, a midwife, and seven country girls, swirling hand in hand under the charts that marked the rise and fall of the satanic seasons, among the symbols of the darker crafts, giddily turning, raising their voices to the roofs as they bowed to the cross reversed above the inner entrance.

Mr Griffiths, half blinded by the staring of the moon, peeped in and saw them. He saw the newborn baby on the cold stones. Unseen in the shadow by the door, he crept towards the baby and lifted it to its feet. The baby fell. Patiently Mr. Griffiths lifted the baby to its feet. But the little mandrake would not walk that night.

The Peaches

The grass-green cart, with 'J. Jones, Gorsehill' painted shakily on
it, stopped in the cobblestone passage between 'The Hare's Foot'
and 'The Pure Drop.' It was late on an April evening. Uncle Jim,
in his black market suit with a stiff white shirt and no collar, loud
new boots, and a plaid cap, creaked and climbed down. He
dragged out a thick wicker basket from a heap of straw in the
corner of the cart and swung it over his shoulder. I heard a squeal
from the basket and saw the tip of a pink tail curling out as Uncle
Jim opened the public door of 'The Pure Drop.'

'I won't be two minutes,' he said to me. The bar was full; two
fat women in bright dresses sat near the door, one with a small
dark child on her knee; they saw Uncle Jim and nudged up on the
bench.

'I'll be out straight away,' he said fiercely, as though I had
contradicted him, 'you stay there quiet.'

The woman without the child raised up her hands. 'Oh, Mr.
Jones,' she said in a high laughing voice. She shook like a jelly.

Then the door closed and the voices were muffled.

I sat alone on the shaft of the cart in the narrow passage, staring
through a side window of 'The Hare's Foot.' A stained blind was
drawn half over it. I could see into half of a smoky, secret room,
where four men were playing cards. One man was huge and
swarthy, with a handlebar moustache and a love-curl on his
forehead; seated by his side was a thin, bald, pale old man with his
cheeks in his mouth; the faces of the other two were in shadow.
They all drank out of brown pint tankards and never spoke, laying
the cards down with a smack, scraping at their match-boxes,
puffing at their pipes, swallowing unhappily, ringing the brass
bell, ordering more, by a sign of the fingers, from a sour woman
with a flowered blouse and a man's cap.

The passage grew dark too suddenly, the walls crowded in,
and the roofs crouched down. To me, staring timidly there in the
dark passage in a strange town, the swarthy man appeared like a

giant in a cage surrounded by clouds, and the bald old man withered into a black hump with a white top; two white hands darted out of the corner with invisible cards. A man with spring-heeled boots and a two-edged knife might be bouncing towards me from Union Street.

I called, 'Uncle Jim, Uncle Jim,' softly so that he should not hear.

I began to whistle between my teeth, but when I stopped I thought the sound went hissing on behind me. I climbed down from the shaft and stepped close to the half-blind window; a hand clawed up the pane to the tassel of the blind; in the little, packed space between me on the cobbles and the card-players at the table, I could not tell which side of the glass was the hand that dragged the blind down slowly. I was cut from the night by a stained square. A story I had made in the warm, safe island of my bed, with sleepy midnight Swansea flowing and rolling round outside the house, came blowing down to me then with a noise on the cobbles. I remembered the demon in the story, with his wings and hooks, who clung like a bat to my hair as I battled up and down Wales after a tall, wise, golden, royal girl from Swansea convent. I tried to remember her true name, her proper, long, black-stockinged legs, her giggle and paper curls, but the hooked wings tore at me and the colour of her hair and eyes faded and vanished like the grass-green of the cart that was a dark, grey mountain now standing between the passage walls.

And all this time the old, broad, patient, nameless mare stood without stirring, not stamping once on the cobbles or shaking her reins. I called her a good girl and stood on tiptoe to try to stroke her ears as the door of 'The Pure Drop' swung open and the warm lamplight from the bar dazzled me and burned my story up. I felt frightened no longer, only angry and hungry. The two fat women near the door giggled 'Good night, Mr. Jones' out of the rich noise and the comfortable smells. The child lay curled asleep under the bench. Uncle Jim kissed the two women on the lips.

'Good night.'

'Good night.'

'Good night.'

Then the passage was dark again.

He backed the mare into Union Street, lurching against her side, cursing her patience and patting her nose, and we both climbed into the cart.

'There are too many drunken gipsies,' he said as we rolled and rattled through the flickering lamp-lit town.

He sang hymns all the way to Gorsehill in an affectionate bass voice, and conducted the wind with his whip. He did not need to touch the reins. Once on the rough road, between hedges twisting out to twig the mare by the bridle and poke our caps, we stopped at a whispered 'Whoa,' for uncle to light his pipe and set the darkness on fire and show his long, red, drunken fox's face to me, with its bristling side-bushes and wet, sensitive nose. A white house with a light in one bedroom window shone in a field on a short hill beyond the road.

Uncle whispered, 'Easy, easy, girl,' to the mare, though she was standing calmly, and said to me over his shoulder in a suddenly loud voice: 'A hangman lived there.'

He stamped on the shaft, and we rattled on through a cutting wind. Uncle shivered, pulling down his cap to hide his ears; but the mare was like a clumsy statue trotting, and all the demons of my stories, if they trotted by her side or crowded together and grinned into her eyes, would not make her shake her head or hurry.

'I wish he'd have hung Mrs. Jesus,' uncle said.

Between hymns he cursed the mare in Welsh. The white house was left behind, the light and the hill were swallowed up.

'Nobody lives there now,' he said.

We drove into the farm-yard of Gorsehill, where the cobbles rang and the black, empty stables took up the ringing and hollowed it so that we drew up in a hollow circle of darkness and the mare was a hollow animal and nothing lived in the hollow house at the end of the yard but two sticks with faces scooped out of turnips.

'You run and see Annie,' said uncle. 'There'll be hot broth and potatoes.'

He led the hollow, shappy statue towards the stable; clop, clop to the mice-house. I heard locks rattle as I ran to the farm-house door.

The front of the house was the single side of a black shell, and the arched door was the listening ear. I pushed the door open and walked into the passage out of the wind. I might have been walking into the hollow night and the wind, passing through a tall vertical shell on an inland sea-shore. Then a door at the end of the passage opened; I saw the plates on the shelves, the lighted lamp on the long, oil-clothed table, 'Prepare to Meet Thy God' knitted over the fire-place, the smiling china dogs, the brown-stained settle, the grandmother clock, and I ran into the kitchen and into Annie's arms.

There was a welcome, then. The clock struck twelve as she kissed me, and I stood among the shining and striking like a prince taking off his disguise. One minute I was small and cold, skulking dead-scared down a black passage in my stiff, best suit, with my hollow belly thumping and my heart like a time bomb, clutching my grammar school cap, unfamiliar to myself, a snub-nosed story-teller lost in his own adventures and longing to be home; the next I was a royal nephew in smart town clothes, embraced and welcomed, standing in the snug centre of my stories and listening to the clock announcing me. She hurried me to the seat in the side of the cavernous fireplace and took off my shoes. The bright lamps and the ceremonial gongs blazed and rang for me.

She made a mustard bath and strong tea, told me to put on a pair of my cousin Gwilym's socks and an old coat of uncle's that smelt of rabbit and tobacco. She fussed and clucked and nodded and told me, as she cut bread and butter, how Gwilym was still studying to be a minister, and how Aunt Rach Morgan, who was ninety years old, had fallen on her belly on a scythe.

Then Uncle Jim came in like the devil with a red face and a wet nose and trembling, hairy hands. His walk was thick. He stumbled against the dresser and shook the coronation plates, and a lean cat shot booted out from the settle corner. Uncle looked nearly twice as tall as Annie. He could have carried her about under his coat and brought her out suddenly, a little, brown-skinned, toothless, hunchbacked woman with a cracked sing-song voice.

'You shouldn't have kept him out so long,' she said, angry and timid.

He sat down in his special chair, which was the broken throne of a bankrupt bard, and lit his pipe and stretched his legs and puffed clouds at the ceiling.

'He might catch his death of cold,' she said.

She talked at the back of his head while he wrapped himself in clouds. The cat slunk back. I sat at the table with my supper finished, and found a little empty bottle and a white balloon in the pockets of my coat.

'Run off to bed, there's a dear,' Annie whispered.

'Can I go and look at the pigs?'

'In the morning, dear,' she said.

So I said good night to Uncle Jim, who turned and smiled at me and winked through the smoke, and I kissed Annie and lit my candle.

'Good night.'

'Good night.'

'Good night.'

I climbed the stairs; each had a different voice. The house smelt of rotten wood and damp and animals. I thought that I had been walking long, damp passages all my life, and climbing stairs in the dark, alone. I stopped outside Gwilym's door on the draughty landing.

'Good night.'

The candle flame jumped in my bedroom where a lamp was burning very low, and the curtains waved; the water in a glass on a round table by the bed stirred, I thought, as the door closed, and lapped against the sides. There was a stream below the window; I thought it lapped against the house all night until I slept.

'Can I go and see the pigs?' I asked Gwilym next morning. The hollow fear of the house was gone, and, running downstairs to my breakfast, I smelt the sweetness of wood and the fresh spring grass and the quiet untidy farm-yard, with its tumbledown dirty-white cow-house and empty stables open.

Gwilym was a tall young man aged nearly twenty, with a thin stick of a body and spade-shaped face. You could dig the garden with him. He had a deep voice that cracked in half when he was excited, and he sang songs to himself, treble and bass, with the same sad hymn tune, and wrote hymns in the barn. He told me stories about girls who died for love. 'And she put a rope round the tree but it was too short,' he said; 'she stuck a pen-knife in her bosoms but it was too blunt.' We were sitting together on the straw heaps that day in the half-dark of the shuttered stable. He twisted and leaned near to me, raising his big finger, and the straw creaked.

'She jumped in the cold river, she jumped,' he said, his mouth against my ear, ' arse over tip and Diu, she was dead.' He squeaked like a bat.

The pigsties were at the far end of the yard. We walked towards them, Gwilym dressed in minister's black, though it was a weekday morning, and me in a serge suit with a darned bottom, past three hens scrabbling the muddy cobbles and a collie with one eye, sleeping with it open. The ramshackle outhouses had tumbling, rotten roofs, jagged holes in their sides, broken shutters, and peeling whitewash; rusty screws ripped out from the dangling, crooked boards; the lean cat of the night before sat snugly between the splintered jaws of bottles, cleaning its face, on the tip of the rubbish pile that rose triangular and smelling sweet and strong to the level of the riddled cart-house roof. There was nowhere like that farm-yard in all the slapdash county, nowhere so poor and grand and dirty as that square of mud and rubbish and bad wood and falling stone, where a bucketful of old and bedraggled hens scratched and laid small eggs. A duck quacked out of the trough in one deserted sty. Now a young man and a curly boy stood staring and sniffing over a wall at a sow, with its tits on the mud, giving suck.

'How many pigs are there?'

'Five. The bitch ate one,' said Gwilym.

We counted them as they squirmed and wriggled, rolled on their backs and bellies, edged and pinched and pushed and squealed about their mother. There were four. We counted again. Four pigs, four naked pink tails curling up as their mouths guzzled down and the sow grunted with pain and joy.

'She must have ate another,' I said, and picked up a scratching stick and prodded the grunting sow and rubbed her crusted bristles backwards. 'Or a fox jumped over the wall,' I said.

'It wasn't the sow or the fox,' said Gwilym. 'It was father.'

I could see uncle, tall and sly and red, holding the writhing pig in his two hairy hands, sinking his teeth in its thigh, crunching its trotters up: I could see him leaning over the wall of the sty with the pig's legs sticking out of his mouth. 'Did Uncle Jim eat the pig?'

Now, at this minute, behind the rotting sheds, he was standing, knee-deep in feathers, chewing off the live heads of the poultry.

'He sold it to go on the drink,' said Gwilym in his deepest rebuking whisper, his eyes fixed on the sky. 'Last Christmas he took a sheep over his shoulder, and he was pissed for ten days.'

The sow rolled nearer the scratching stick, and the small pigs sucking at her, lost and squealing in the sudden darkness, struggled under her folds and pouches.

'Come and see my chapel,' said Gwilym. He forgot the lost pig at once and began to talk about the towns he had visited on a religious tour, Neath and Bridgend and Bristol and Newport, with their lakes and luxury gardens, their bright, coloured streets roaring with temptation. We walked away from the sty and the disappointed sow.

'I met actress after actress,' he said.

Gwilym's chapel was the last old barn before the field that led down to the river; it stood well above the farm-yard, on a mucky hill. There was one whole door with a heavy padlock, but you could get in easily through the holes on either side of it. He took out a ring of keys and shook them gently and tried each one in the lock. 'Very posh,' he said; 'I bought them from the junk-shop in Carmarthen.' We climbed into the chapel through a hole.

A dusty wagon with the name painted out and a white-wash cross on its side stood in the middle. 'My pulpit cart,' he said, and walked solemnly into it up the broken shaft. 'You sit on the hay; mind the mice,' he said. Then he brought out his deepest voice again, and cried to the heavens and the bat-lined rafters and the hanging webs: 'Bless us this holy day, O Lord, bless me and Dylan and this Thy little chapel for ever and ever, Amen. I've done a lot of improvements to this place.'

I sat on the hay and stared at Gwilym preaching, and heard his voice rise and crack and sink to a whisper and break into singing and Welsh and ring triumphantly and be wild and meek. The sun through a hole, shone on his praying shoulders, and he said: 'O God, Thou art everywhere all the time, in the dew of the morning, in the frost of the evening, in the field and the town, in the preacher and the sinner, in the sparrow and the big buzzard. Thou canst see everything, right down deep in our hearts; Thou canst see us when the sun is gone; Thou canst see us when there aren't any stars, in the gravy blackness, in the deep, deep, deep, deep pit; Thou canst see and spy and watch us all the time, in the little black corners, in the big cowboys' prairies, under the blankets when we're snoring fast, in the terrible shadows; pitch black, pitch black; Thou canst see everything we do, in the night and day, in the day and the night, everything, everything; Thou canst see all the time. O God, mun, you're like a bloody cat.'

He let his clasped hands fall. The chapel in the barn was still, and shafted with sunlight. There was nobody to cry Hallelujah or God-bless; I was too small and enamoured in the silence. The one duck quacked outside.

'Now I take a collection,' Gwilym said.

He stepped down from the cart and groped about in the hay beneath it and held out a battered tin to me.

'I haven't got a proper box,' he said.

I put two pennies in the tin.

'It's time for dinner,' he said, and we went back to the house without a word.

Annie said, when we had finished dinner: 'Put on your nice suit for this afternoon. The one with stripes.'

It was to be a special afternoon, for my best friend, Jack Williams, from Swansea, was coming down with his rich mother in a motor car, and Jack was to spend a fortnight's holiday with me.

'Where's Uncle Jim?'

'He's gone to market,' said Annie.

Gwilym made a small pig's noise. We knew where uncle was; he was sitting in a public house with a heifer over his shoulder and two pigs nosing out of his pockets, and his lips wet with bull's blood.

'Is Mrs. Williams very rich?' asked Gwilym.

I told him she had three motor cars and two houses, which was a lie. 'She's the richest woman in Wales, and once she was a mayoress,' I said. 'Are we going to have tea in the best room?'

Annie nodded. 'And a large tin of peaches,' she said.

'That old tin's been in the cupboard since Christmas,' said Gwilym, 'mother's been keeping it for a day like this.'

'They're lovely peaches,' Annie said. She went upstairs to dress like Sunday.

The best room smelt of moth balls and fur and damp and dead plants and stale, sour air. Two glass cases on wooden coffin-boxes lined the window wall. You looked at the weed-grown vegetable garden through a stuffed fox's legs, over a partridge's head, along the red-paint-stained breast of a stiff wild duck. A case of china and pewter, trinkets, teeth, family brooches, stood beyond the bandy table; there was a large oil lamp on the patchwork table-cloth, a Bible with a clasp, a tall vase with a draped woman about to bathe on it, and a framed photograph of Annie, Uncle Jim, and Gwilym smiling in front of a fern-pot. On the mantelpiece were two clocks, some dogs, brass candlesticks, a shepherdess, a man in a kilt, and a tinted photograph of Annie, with high hair and her breasts coming out. There were chairs around the table and in each corner, straight, curved, stained, padded, all with lace cloths hanging over their backs. A patched white sheet shrouded the harmonium. The fireplace was full of brass tongs, shovels, and pokers. The best room was rarely used. Annie dusted and brushed and polished there once a week, but the carpet still sent up a grey cloud when you trod on it, and dust lay evenly on the seats of the chairs, and balls of cotton and dirt and black stuffing and long black horse hairs were wedged in the cracks of the sofa. I blew on the glass to see the pictures. Gwilym and castles and cattle.

'Change your suit now,' said Gwilym.

I wanted to wear my old suit, to look like a proper farm boy and have manure in my shoes and hear it squelch as I walked, to see a cow have calves and a bull on top of a cow, to run down in the dingle and wet my stockings, to go out and shout, 'Come on, you b——,' and pelt the hens and talk in a proper voice. But I went upstairs to put my striped suit on.

From my bedroom I heard the noise of a motor car drawing up the yard. It was Jack Williams and his mother.

Gwilym shouted, 'They're here, in a Daimler!' from the foot of the stairs, and I ran down to meet them with my tie undone and my hair uncombed.

Annie was saying at the door: 'Good afternoon, Mrs. Williams, good afternoon. Come right in, it's a lovely day, Mrs. Williams. Did you have a nice journey then? This way, Mrs. Williams, mind the step.'

Annie wore a black, shining dress that smelt of moth balls, like the chair covers in the best room; she had forgotten to change her gym-shoes, which were caked with mud and all holes. She fussed on before Mrs. Williams down the stone passage, darting her head round, clucking, fidgeting, excusing the small house, anxiously tidying her hair with one rough, stubby hand.

Mrs. Williams was tall and stout, with a jutting bosom and thick legs, her ankles swollen over her pointed shoes; she was fitted out like a mayoress or a ship, and she swayed after Annie into the best room.

She said: 'Please don't put yourself out for me, Mrs. Jones, there's a dear.' She dusted the seat of a chair with a lace handkerchief from her bag before sitting down.

'I can't stop, you know,' she said.

'Oh, you must stay for a cup of tea,' said Annie, shifting and scraping the chairs away from the table so that nobody could move and Mrs. Williams was hemmed in fast with her bosom and her rings and her bag, opening the china cupboard, upsetting the Bible on the floor, picking it up, dusting it hurriedly with her sleeve.

'And peaches,' Gwilym said. He was standing in the passage with his hat on.

Annie said, 'Take your hat off, Gwilym, make Mrs. Williams comfortable,' and she put the lamp on the shrouded harmonium and spread out a white table-cloth that had a tea stain in the centre, and brought out the china and laid knives and cups for five.

'Don't bother about me, there's a dear,' said Mrs. Williams. 'There's a lovely fox!' She flashed a finger of rings at the glass case.

'It's real blood,' I told Jack, and we climbed over the sofa to the table.

'No, it isn't,' he said, 'it's red ink.'

'Oh, your shoes!' said Annie.

'Don't tread on the sofa, Jack, there's a dear.'

'If it isn't ink it's paint then.'

Gwilym said: 'Shall I get you a bit of cake, Mrs. Williams?'

Annie rattled the tea-cups. 'There isn't a single bit of cake in the house,' she said; 'we forgot to order it from the shop; not a single bit. Oh, Mrs. Williams!'

Mrs. Williams said: 'Just a cup of tea thanks.' She was still sweating because she had walked all the way from the car. It spoiled her powder. She sparkled her rings and dabbed at her face.

'Three lumps,' she said. 'And I'm sure Jack will be very happy here.'

'Happy as sandboys.' Gwilym sat down.

'Now you must have some peaches, Mrs. Williams, they're lovely.'

'They should be, they've been here long enough,' said Gwilym.

Annie rattled the tea-cups at him again.

'No peaches, thanks,' Mrs. Williams said.

'Oh, you must, Mrs. Williams, just one. With cream.'

'No, no, Mrs. Jones, thanks the same,' she said. 'I don't mind pears or chunks, but I can't bear peaches.'

Jack and I had stopped talking. Annie stared down at her gym-shoes. One of the clocks on the mantelpiece coughed, and struck. Mrs. Williams struggled from her chair.

'There, time flies!' she said.

She pushed her way past the furniture, jostled against the sideboard, rattled the trinkets and brooches, and kissed Jack on the forehead.

'You've got scent on,' he said.

She patted my head.

'Now behave yourselves.'

To Annie, she said in a whisper: 'And remember, Mrs. Jones, just good plain food. No spoiling his appetite.'

Annie followed her out of the room. She moved slowly now. 'I'll do my very best, Mrs. Williams.'

We heard her say, 'Good-bye then, Mrs. Williams,' and go down the steps of the kitchen and close the door. The motor car roared in the yard, then the noise grew softer and died.

Down the thick dingle Jack and I ran shouting, scalping the brambles with our thin stick-hatchets, dancing, hallooing. We skidded to a stop and prowled on the bushy banks of the stream. Up above, sat one-eyed, dead-eyed, sinister, slim, ten-notched Gwilym, loading his guns in Gallows Farm. We crawled and rat-tatted through the bushes, hid, at a whistled signal, in the deep grass, and crouched there, waiting for the crack of a twig or the secret breaking of boughs.

On my haunches, eager and alone, casting an ebony shadow, with the Gorsehill jungle swarming, the violent, impossible birds and fishes leaping, hidden under four-stemmed flowers the height of horses, in the early evening in a dingle near Carmarthen, my friend Jack Williams invisibly near me, I felt all my young body like an excited animal surrounding me, the torn knees bent, the bumping heart, the long heat and depth between the legs, the sweat prickling in the hands, the tunnels down to the eardrums, the little balls of dirt between the toes, the eyes in the sockets, the tucked-up voice, the blood racing, the memory around and within flying, jumping, swimming, and waiting to pounce. There, playing Indians in the evening, I was aware of me myself in the exact middle of a living story, and my body was my adventure and my name. I sprang with excitement and scrambled up through the scratching brambles again.

Jack cried: 'I see you! I see you!' He scampered after me. 'Bang! bang! you're dead!'

But I was young and loud and alive, though I lay down obediently.

'Now you try and kill me,' said Jack. 'Count a hundred.'

I closed one eye, saw him rush and stamp towards the upper field, then tiptoe back and begin to climb a tree, and I counted fifty and ran to the foot of the tree and killed him as he climbed. 'You fall down,' I said.

He refused to fall, so I climbed too, and we clung to the top branches and stared down at the lavatory in the corner of the field. Gwilym was sitting on the seat with his trousers down. He looked small and black. He was reading a book and moving his hands.

'We can see you!' we shouted.

He snatched his trousers up and put the book in his pocket.

'We can see you, Gwilym!'

He came out into the field. 'Where are you, then?'

We waved our caps at him.

'In the sky!' Jack shouted.

'Flying!' I shouted.

We stretched our arms out like wings.

'Fly down here.'

We swung and laughed on the branches.

'There's birds!' cried Gwilym.

Our jackets were torn and our stockings were wet and our shoes were sticky; we had green moss and brown bark on our hands and faces when we went in for supper and a scolding. Annie was quiet that night, though she called me a ragamuffin and said she didn't know what Mrs. Williams would think and told Gwilym he should know better. We made faces at Gwilym and put salt in his tea, but after supper he said: 'You can come to the chapel if you like. Just before bed.'

He lit a candle on the top of the pulpit cart. It was a small light in the big barn. The bats were gone. Shadows still clung upside down along the roof. Gwilym was no longer my cousin in a Sunday suit, but a tall stranger shaped like a spade in a cloak, and his voice grew too deep. The straw heaps were lively. I thought of the sermon on the cart: we were watched, Jack's heart was watched, Gwilym's tongue was marked down, my whisper, 'Look at the little eyes,' was remembered always.

'Now I take confessions,' said Gwilym from the cart.

Jack and I stood bareheaded in the circle of the candle, and I could feel the trembling of Jack's body.

'You first.' Gwilym's finger, as bright as though he had held it in the candle flame until it burned, pointed me out, and I took a step towards the pulpit cart, raising my head.

'Now you confess,' said Gwilym.

'What have I got to confess?'

'The worst thing you've done.'

I let Edgar Reynolds be whipped because I had taken his homework; I stole from my mother's bag; I stole from Gwyneth's bag; I stole twelve books in three visits from the library, and threw them away in the park; I drank a cup of my water to see what it tasted like; I beat a dog with a stick so that it would roll over and lick my hand afterwards; I looked with Dan Jones through the keyhole while his maid had a bath; I cut my knee with a penknife, and put the blood on my handkerchief and said it had come out of my ears so that I could pretend I was ill and frighten my mother; I pulled my trousers down and showed Jack Williams; I saw Billy Jones beat a pigeon to death with a fire-shovel, and laughed and got sick; Cedric Williams and I broke into Mrs. Samuels' house and poured ink over the bedclothes.

I said: 'I haven't done anything bad.'

'Go on, confess,' said Gwilym. He was frowning down at me.

'I can't! I can't!' I said. 'I haven't done anything bad.'

'Go on, confess!'

'I won't! I won't!'

Jack began to cry. 'I want to go home,' he said.

Gwilym opened the chapel door and we followed him into the yard, down past the black, humped sheds, towards the house, and Jack sobbed all the way.

In bed together, Jack and I confessed our sins.

'I steal from my mother's bag, too; there are pounds and pounds.'

'How much do you steal?'

'Threepence.'

'I killed a man once.'

'No you didn't then.'

'Honest to Christ, I shot him through the heart.'

'What was his name?'

'Williams.'

'Did he bleed?'

I thought the stream was lapping against the house.

'Like a bloody pig,' I said.

Jack's tears had dried. 'I don't like Gwilym, he's barmy.'

'No he isn't. I found a lot of poems in his bedroom once. They were all written to girls. And he showed them to me afterwards, and he'd changed all the girls' names to God.'

'He's religious.'

'No he isn't, he goes with actresses. He knows Corinne Griffith.'

Our door was open. I liked the door locked at night, because I would rather have a ghost in the bedroom than think of one coming in; but Jack liked it open, and we tossed and he won. We heard the front door rattle and footsteps in the kitchen passage.

'That's Uncle Jim.'

'What's he like?'

'He's like a fox, he eats pigs and chickens.'

The ceiling was thin and we heard every sound, the creaking of the bard's chair, the clatter of plates, Annie's voice saying: 'Midnight!'

'He's drunk,' I said. We lay quite still, hoping to hear a quarrel.

'Perhaps he'll throw plates,' I said.

But Annie scolded him softly. 'There's a fine state, Jim.'

He murmured to her.

'There's one pig gone,' she said. 'Oh, why do you have to do it, Jim? There's nothing left now. We'll never be able to carry on.'

'Money! money! money!' he said. I knew he would be lighting his pipe.

Then Annie's voice grew so soft we could not hear the words, and uncle said: 'Did she pay you the thirty shillings?'

'They're talking about your mother,' I told Jack.

For a long time Annie spoke in a low voice, and we waited for words. 'Mrs. Williams,' she said, and 'motor car,' and 'Jack,' and 'peaches.' I thought she was crying for her voice broke on the last word.

Uncle Jim's chair creaked again, he might have struck his fist on the table, and we heard him shout: 'I'll give her peaches! Peaches, peaches! Who does she think she is? Aren't peaches good enough for her? To hell with her bloody motor car and her bloody son! Making us small.'

'Don't, don't Jim!' Annie said, 'you'll wake the boys.'

'I'll wake them and whip the hell out of them, too!'

'Please, please, Jim!'

'You send the boy away,' he said, 'or I'll do it myself. Back to his three bloody houses.'

Jack pulled the bedclothes over his head and sobbed into the pillow: 'I don't want to hear, I don't want to hear. I'll write to my mother. She'll take me away.'

I climbed out to close the door. Jack would not talk to me again, and I fell asleep to the noise of the voices below, which soon grew gentle.

Uncle Jim was not at breakfast. When we came down, Jack's shoes were cleaned for him and his jacket was darned and pressed. Annie gave two boiled eggs to Jack and one to me. She forgave me when I drank tea from the saucer.

After breakfast, Jack walked to the post office. I took the one-eyed collie to chase rabbits in the upper fields, but it barked at ducks and brought me a tramp's shoe from a hedge, and lay down with its tail wagging in a rabbit hole. I threw stones at the deserted duck pond, and the collie ambled back with sticks.

Jack went skulking into the damp dingle, his hands in his pockets, his cap over one eye. I left the collie sniffing at a molehill, and climbed to the tree-top in the corner of the lavatory field. Below me, Jack was playing Indians all alone, scalping through the bushes, surprising himself round a tree, hiding from himself in the grass. I called to him once, but he pretended not to hear. He played alone, silently and savagely. I saw him standing with his hands in his pockets, swaying like a Kelly, on the mudbank by the stream at the foot of the dingle. My bough lurched, the heads of the dingle bushes spun up towards me like green tops, 'I'm falling!' I cried, my trousers saved me, I swung and grasped, this was one minute of wild adventure, but Jack did not look up and the minute was lost. I climbed, without dignity, to the ground.

Early in the afternoon, after a silent meal, when Gwilym was reading the scriptures or writing hymns to girls or sleeping in his chapel, Annie was baking bread, and I was cutting a wooden whistle in the loft over the stable, the motor car drove up in the yard again.

Out of the house Jack, in his best suit, ran to meet his mother, and I heard him say as she stepped, raising her short skirts, on to the cobbles: 'And he called you a bloody cow, and he said he'd whip the hell out of me, and Gwilym took me to the barn in the dark and let the mice run over me, and Dylan's a thief, and that old woman's spoilt my jacket.'

Mrs. Williams sent the chauffeur for Jack's luggage. Annie came to the door, trying to smile and curtsy, tidying her hair, wiping her hands on her pinafore.

Mrs. Williams said, 'Good afternoon,' and sat with Jack in the back of the car and stared at the ruin of Gorsehill.

The chauffeur came back. The car drove off, scattering the hens. I ran out of the stable to wave to Jack. He sat still and stiff by his mother's side. I waved my handkerchief.

Just Like Little Dogs

Standing alone under a railway arch out of the wind, I was looking at the miles of sands, long and dirty in the early dark, with only a few boys on the edge of the sea and one or two hurrying couples with their mackintoshes blown around them like balloons, when two young men joined me, it seemed out of nowhere, and struck matches for their cigarettes and illuminated their faces under bright-checked caps.

One had a pleasant face; his eyebrows slanted comically towards his temples, his eyes were warm, brown, deep, and guileless, and his mouth was full and weak. The other man had a boxer's nose and a weighted chin ginger with bristles.

We watched the boys returning from the oily sea; they shouted under the echoing arch, then their voices faded. Soon there was not a single couple in sight; the lovers had disappeared among the sandhills and were lying down there with broken tins and bottles of the summer passed, old paper blowing by them, and nobody with any sense was about. The strangers, huddled against the wall, their hands deep in their pockets, their cigarettes sparkling, stared, I thought, at the thickening of the dark over the empty sands, but their eyes may have been closed. A train raced over us, and the arch shook. Over the shore, behind the vanishing train, smoke clouds flew together, rags of wings and hollow bodies of great birds black as tunnels, and broke up lazily; cinders fell through a sieve in the air, and the sparks were put out by the wet dark before they reached the sand. The night before, little quick scarecrows had bent and picked at the track-line and a solitary dignified scavenger wandered three miles by the edge with a crumpled coal sack and a park-keeper's steel-tipped stick. Now they were tucked up in sacks, asleep in a siding, their heads in bins, their beards in straw, in coal-trucks thinking of fires, or lying beyond pickings on Jack Stiff's slab near the pub in the Fishguard Alley, where the methylated-spirit drinkers danced into the policemen's arms and women like lumps of clothes in a pool waited, in doorways and holes in the soaking wall, for vampires or firemen. Night was properly down on us now. The wind changed. Thin rain began. The sands themselves went out. We stood in the scooped, windy room of the arch, listening to the noises from the muffled town, a goods train shunting, a siren in the docks, the hoarse trams in the streets far behind, one bark of a dog, unplaceable sounds, iron being beaten, the distant creaking of wood, doors slamming where there were no houses, an engine coughing like a sheep on a hill.

The two young men were statues smoking, tough-capped and collarless watchers and witnesses carved out of the stone of the blowing room where they stood at my side with nowhere to go, nothing to do, and all the raining, almost winter, night before them. I cupped a match to let them see my face in a dramatic shadow, my eyes mysteriously sunk, perhaps, in a startling white face, my young looks savage in the sudden flicker of light, to make them wonder who I was as I puffed my last butt and puzzled about them. Why was the soft-faced young man, with his tame devil's eyebrows, standing like a stone figure with a glow-worm in it? He should have a nice girl to bully him gently and take him to cry in the pictures, or kids to bounce in a kitchen in Rodney Street. There was no sense in standing silent for hours under a railway arch on a hell of a night at the end of a bad summer when girls were waiting, ready to be hot and friendly, in chip shops and shop doorways and Rabbiotti's all-night café, when the public bar of the 'Bay View' at the corner had a fire and skittles and a swarthy, sensuous girl with different coloured eyes, when the billiard saloons were open, except the one in High Street you couldn't go into without a collar and tie, when the closed parks had empty, covered bandstands and the railings were easy to climb.

A church clock somewhere struck a lot, faintly from the night on the right, but I didn't count.

The other young man, less than two feet from me, should be shouting with the boys, boasting in lanes, propping counters, prancing and clouting in the Mannesmann Hall, or whispering around a bucket in a ring corner. Why was he humped here with a moody man and myself, listening to our breathing, to the sea, the wind scattering sand through the archway, a chained dog and a foghorn and the rumble of trams a dozen streets away, watching a match strike, a boy's fresh face spying in a shadow, the lighthouse beams, the movement of a hand to a fag, when the sprawling town in a drizzle, the pubs and the clubs and the coffee-shops, the prowlers' streets, the arches near the promenade, were full of friends and enemies? He could be playing nap by a candle in a shed in a wood-yard.

Families sat down to supper in rows of short houses, the wireless sets were on, the daughters' young men sat in the front rooms. In neighbouring houses they read the news off the table-cloth, and the potatoes from dinner were fried up. Cards were played in the front rooms of houses on the hills. In the houses on tops of the hills families were entertaining friends, and the blinds of the front rooms were not quite drawn. I heard the sea in a cold bit of the cheery night.

One of the strangers said suddenly, in a high, clear voice: 'What are we all doing then?'

'Standing under a bloody arch,' said the other one.

'And it's cold,' I said.

'It isn't very cosy,' said the high voice of the young man with the pleasant face, now invisible. 'I've been in better hotels than this.'

'What about that night in the Majestic?' said the other voice.

There was a long silence.

'Do you often stand here?' said the pleasant man. His voice might never have broken.

'No, this is the first time here,' I said. 'Sometimes I stand in the Brynmill arch.'

'Ever tried the old pier?'

'It's no good in the rain, is it?'

'Underneath the pier, I mean, in the girders.'

'No, I haven't been there.'

'Tom spends every Sunday under the pier,' the pug-faced young man said bitterly. 'I got to take him his dinner in a piece of paper.'

'There's another train coming,' I said. It tore over us, the arch bellowed, the wheels screamed through our heads, we were deafened and spark-blinded and crushed under the fiery weight and we rose again, like battered black men, in the grave of the arch. No noise at all from the swallowed town. The trams had rattled themselves dumb. A pressure of the hidden sea rubbed away the smudge of the docks. Only three young men were alive.

One said: 'It's a sad life, without a home.'

'Haven't you got a home then?' I said.

'Oh, yes, I've got a home all right.'

'I got one, too.'

'And I live near Cwmdonkin Park,' I said.

'That's another place Tom sits in in the dark. He says he listens to the owls.'

'I knew a chap once who lived in the country, near Bridgend,' said Tom, 'and they had a munition works there in the War and it spoiled all the birds. The chap I know says you can always tell a cuckoo from Bridgend, it goes:"Cuckbloodyoo! cuckbloodyoo!"'

'Cuckbloodyoo!' echoed the arch.

'Why are you standing under the arch, then?' asked Tom. 'It's warm at home. You can draw the curtains and sit by the fire, snug as a bug. Gracie's on the wireless to-night. No shananacking in the old moonlight.'

'I don't want to go home, I don't want to sit by the fire. I've got nothing to do when I'm in and I don't want to go to bed. I like standing about like this with nothing to do, in the dark all by myself,' I said.

And I did, too. I was a lonely nightwalker and a steady stander-at-corners. I liked to walk through the wet town after midnight, when the streets were deserted and the window lights out, alone and alive on the glistening tramlines in dead and empty High Street under the moon, gigantically sad in the damp streets by ghostly Ebenezer Chapel. And I never felt more a part of the remote and overpressing world, or more full of love and arrogance and pity and humility, not for myself alone, but for the living earth I suffered on and for the unfeeling systems in the upper air, Mars and Venus and Brazell and Skully, men in China and St. Thomas, scorning girls and ready girls, soldiers and bullies and policemen and sharp, suspicious buyers of second-hand books, bad, ragged women who'd pretend against the museum wall for a cup of tea, and perfect, unapproachable women out of the fashion magazines, seven feet high, sailing slowly in their flat, glazed creations through steel and glass and velvet. I leant against the wall of a derelict house in the residential areas or wandered in the empty rooms, stood terrified on the stairs or gazing through the smashed windows at the sea or at nothing, and the lights going out one by one in the avenues. Or I mooched in a half-built house, with the sky stuck in the roof and cats on the ladders and a wind shaking through the bare bones of the bedrooms.

'And you can talk,' I said. 'Why aren't you at home?'

'I don't want to be home,' said Tom.

'I'm not particular,' said his friend.

When a match flared, their heads rocked and spread on the wall, and shapes of winged bulls and buckets grew bigger and smaller. Tom began to tell a story. I thought of a new stranger walking on the sands past the arch and hearing all of a sudden that high voice out of a hole.

I missed the beginning of the story as I thought of the man on the sands listening in a panic or dodging, like a footballer, in and out among the jumping dark towards the lights behind the railway line, and remembered Tom's voice in the middle of a sentence.

'... went up to them and said it was a lovely night. It wasn't a lovely night at all. The sands were empty. We asked them what their names were and they asked us what ours were. We were walking along by this time. Walter here was telling them about the glee party in the "Melba" and what went on in the ladies' cloakroom. You had to drag the tenors away like ferrets.'

'What were their names?' I asked.

'Doris and Norma,' Walter said.

'So we walked along the sands towards the dunes,' Tom said, 'and Walter was with Doris and I was with Norma. Norma worked in the steam laundry. We hadn't been walking and talking for more than a few minutes when, by God, I knew I was head over heels in love with the girl, and she wasn't the pretty one, either.'

He described her. I saw her clearly. Her plump, kind face, jolly brown eyes, warm wide mouth, thick bobbed hair, rough body, bottle legs, broad bum, grew from a few words right out of Tom's story, and I saw her ambling solidly along the sands in a spotted frock in a showering autumn evening with fancy gloves on her hard hands, a gold bangle, with a voile handkerchief tucked in it, round her wrist, and a navy-blue handbag with letters and outing snaps, a compact, a bus ticket, and a shilling.

'Doris was the pretty one,' said Tom, 'smart and touched up and sharp as a knife. I was twenty-six years old and I'd never been in love, and there I was, gawking at Norma in the middle of Tawe sands, too frightened to put my finger on her gloves. Walter had his arm round Doris then.'

They sheltered behind a dune. The night dropped down on them quickly. Walter was a caution with Doris, hugging and larking, and Tom sat close to Norma, brave enough to hold her hand in its cold glove and tell her all his secrets. He told her his age and his job. He liked staying in in the evenings with a good book.

Norma liked dances. He liked dances, too. Norma and Doris were sisters. 'I'd never have thought that,' Tom said, 'you're beautiful, I love you.'

Now the story-telling thing in the arch gave place to the loving night in the dunes. The arch was as high as the sky. The faint town noises died. I lay like a pimp in a bush by Tom's side and squinted through to see him round his hands on Norma's breast. 'Don't you dare!' Walter and Doris lay quietly near them. You could have heard a safety-pin fall.

'And the curious thing was,' said Tom, 'that after a time we all sat up on the sand and smiled at each other. And then we all moved softly about on the sand in the dark, without saying a word. And Doris was lying with me, and Norma was with Walter.'

'But why did you change over, if you loved her?' I asked.

'I never understood why,' said Tom. 'I think about it every night.'

'That was in October,' Walter said.

And Tom continued: 'We didn't see much of the girls until July. I couldn't face Norma. Then they brought two paternity orders against us, and Mr. Lewis, the magistrate, was eighty years old, and stone deaf, too. He put a little trumpet by his ear and Norma and Doris gave evidence. Then we gave evidence, and he couldn't decide whose was which. And at the end he shook his head back and fore and pointed his trumpet and said: "Just like little dogs!"'

All at once I remembered how cold it was. I rubbed my numb hands together. Fancy standing all night in the cold. Fancy listening, I thought, to a long, unsatisfactory story in the frost-bite night in a polar arch. 'What happened then?' I asked.

Walter answered. 'I married Norma,' he said 'and Tom married Doris. We had to do the right thing by them, didn't we? That's why Tom won't go home. He never goes home till the early morning. I've got to keep him company. He's my brother.'

It would take me ten minutes to run home. I put up my coat collar and pulled my cap down.

'And the curious thing is,' said Tom, 'that I love Norma and Walter doesn't love Norma or Doris. We've two nice little boys. I call mine Norman.'

We all shook hands.

'See you again,' said Walter.

'I'm always hanging about,' said Tom.

'Abyssinia!'

I walked out of the arch, crossed Trafalgar Terrace, and pelted up the steep streets.

Old Garbo

Mr. Farr trod delicately and disgustedly down the dark, narrow stairs like a man on ice. He knew, without looking or slipping, that vicious boys had littered the darkest corners with banana peel; and when he reached the lavatory, the basins would be choked and the chains snapped on purpose. He remembered 'Mr. Farr, no father' scrawled in brown, and the day the sink was full of blood that nobody admitted having lost. A girl rushed past him up the stairs, knocked the papers out of his hand, did not apologize, and the loose meg of his cigarette burned his lower lip as he failed to open the lavatory door. I heard from inside his protest and rattlings, the sing-song whine of his voice, the stamping of his small patent-leather shoes, his favourite swear-words—he swore, violently and privately, like a collier used to thinking in the dark—and I let him in.

'Do you always lock the door?' he asked, scurrying to the tiled wall.

'It stuck,' I said.

He shivered, and buttoned.

He was the senior reporter, a great shorthand writer, a chain-smoker, a bitter drinker, very humorous, round-faced and round-bellied, with dart holes in his nose. Once, I thought as I stared at him then in the lavatory of the offices of the *Tawe News*, he might have been a mincing-mannered man, with a strut and a cane to balance it, a watch-chain across the waistcoat, a gold tooth, even, perhaps a flower from his own garden in his buttonhole. But now each attempt at a precise gesture was caked and soaked before it began; when he placed the tips of his thumb and forefinger together, you saw only the cracked nails in mourning and the Woodbine stains. He gave me a cigarette and shook his coat to hear matches.

'Here's a light, Mr. Farr,' I said.

It was good to keep in with him; he covered all the big stories, the occasional murder, such as when Thomas O'Connor used a bottle on his wife—but that was before my time—the strikes, the best fires. I wore my cigarette as he did, a hanging badge of bad habits.

'Look at that word on the wall,' he said. 'Now that's ugly. There's a time and a place.'

Winking at me, scratching his bald patch as though the thought came from there, he said: 'Mr. Solomon wrote that.'

Mr. Solomon was the news editor and a Wesleyan.

'Old Solomon,' said Mr. Farr, 'he'd cut every baby in half just for pleasure.'

I smiled and said: 'I bet he would!' But I wished that I could have answered in such a way as to show for Mr. Solomon the disrespect I did not feel. This was a great male moment, and the most enjoyable since I had begun work three weeks before: leaning against the cracked tiled wall, smoking and smiling, looking down at my shoe scraping circles on the wet floor, sharing a small wickedness with an old, important man. I should have been writing up last night's performance of *The Crucifixion* or loitering, with my new hat on one side, through the Christmas-Saturday-crowded town in the hopes of an accident.

'You must come along with me one night,' Mr. Farr said slowly. 'We'll go down the "Fishguard" on the docks; you can see the sailors knitting there in the public bar. Why not tonight? And there's shilling women in the "Lord Jersey." You stick to Woodbines, like me.'

He washed his hands as a young boy does, wiping the dirt on the roll-towel, stared in the mirror over the basin, twirled the ends of his moustache, and saw them droop again immediately after.

'Get to work,' he said.

I walked into the lobby, leaving him with his face pressed to the glass and one finger exploring his bushy nostrils.

It was nearly eleven o'clock, and time for a cocoa or a Russian tea in the Café Royal, above the tobacconist's in High Street, where junior clerks and shop assistants and young men working in their fathers' offices or articled to stock brokers and solicitors meet every morning for gossip and stories. I made my way through the crowds: the Valley men, up for the football; the country shoppers, the window gazers; the silent, shabby men at the corners of the packed streets, standing in isolation in the rain; the press of mothers and prams; old women in black, brooched dresses carrying frails, smart girls with shining mackintoshes and splashed stockings; little, dandy lascars, bewildered by the weather; business men with wet spats; through a mushroom forest of umbrellas; and all the time I thought of the paragraphs I would never write. I'll put you all in a story by and by.

Mrs. Constable, laden and red with shopping, recognized me as she charged out of Woolworth's like a bull. 'I haven't seen your mother for ages! Oh! this Christmas rush! Remember me to Florrie. I'm going to have a cup of tea at the "Modern." There,' she said, 'I've lost a pan!'

I saw Percy Lewis, who put chewing gum in my hair at school.

A tall man stared at the doorway of a hat shop, resisting the crowds, standing hard and still. All the moving irrelevancies of good news grew and acted around me as I reached the café entrance and climbed the stairs.

'What's for you, Mr. Swaffer?'

'The usual, please.' Cocoa and free biscuit.

Most of the boys were there already. Some wore the outlines of moustaches, others had sideboards and crimped hair, some smoked curved pipes and talked with them gripped between their teeth, there were pin-stripe trousers and hard collars, one daring bowler.

'Sit by here,' said Leslie Bird. He was in the boots at Dan Lewis's.

'Been to the flicks this week, Thomas?'

'Yes. The Regal. *White Lies*. Damned good show, too! Connie Bennett was great! Remember her in the foam-bath, Leslie?'

'Too much foam for me, old man.'

The broad vowels of the town were narrowed in, the rise and fall of the family accent was caught and pressed.

At the top window of the International Stores across the street a group of uniformed girls were standing with tea-cups in their hands. One of them waved a handkerchief. I wondered if she waved it to me. 'There's that dark piece again,' I said. 'She's got her eye on you.'

'They look all right in their working clothes,' he said. 'You catch them when they're all dolled up, they're awful. I knew a little nurse once, she looked a peach in her uniform, really refined; no, really, I mean. I picked her up on the prom one night. She was in her Sunday best. There's a difference; she looked like a bit of Marks and Spencer's.' As he talked he was looking through the window with the corners of his eyes.

The girl waved again, and turned away to giggle.

'Pretty cheap!' he said.

I said: 'And little Audrey laughed and laughed.'

He took out a plated cigarette case. 'Present,' he said. 'I bet my uncle with three balls has it in a week. Have a best Turkish.'

His matches were marked Allsopps. 'Got them from the "Carlton"' he said. 'Pretty girl behind the bar: knows her onions. You've never been there, have you? Why don't you drop in for one to-night? Gil Morris'll be there, too. We usually sink a couple Saturdays. There's a hop at the "Melba."'

'Sorry,' I said. 'I'm going out with our senior reporter. Some other time, Leslie. So long!'

I paid my threepence.

'Good morning, Cassie.'

'Good morning, Hannen.'

The rain had stopped and High Street shone. Walking on the tram-lines, a neat man held his banner high and prominently feared the Lord. I knew him as a Mr. Matthews, who had been saved some years ago from British port and who now walked every night, in rubber shoes with a prayer book and a flashlight, through the lanes. There went Mr. Evans the Produce through the side-door of the 'Bugle.' Three typists rushed by for lunch, poached egg and milk-shake, leaving a lavender scent. Should I take the long way through the Arcade, and stop to look at the old man with the broken, empty pram who always stood there, by the music store, and who would take off his cap and set his hair alight for a penny? It was only a trick to amuse boys, and I took the short cut down Chapel Street, on the edge of the slum called the Strand, past the enticing Italian chip shop where young men who had noticing parents bought twopennyworth on late nights to hide their breath before the last tram home. Then up the narrow office stairs and into the reporters' room.

Mr. Solomon was shouting down the telephone. I heard the last words: 'You're just a dreamer, Williams.' He put the receiver down. 'That boy's a buddy dreamer,' he said to no one. He never swore.

I finished my report of *The Crucifixion* and handed it to Mr. Farr.

'Too much platitudinous verbosity.'

Half an hour later, Ted Williams, dressed to golf, sidled in, smiling, thumbed his nose at Mr. Solomon's back, and sat quietly in a corner with a nail-file.

I whispered: 'What was he slanging you for?'

'I went out on a suicide, a tram conductor called Hopkins, and the widow made me stay and have a cup of tea. That's all.' He was very winning in his ways, more like a girl than a man who dreamed of Fleet Street and spent his summer fortnight walking up and down past the *Daily Express* and looking for celebrities in the pubs.

Saturday was my free afternoon. It was one o'clock and time to leave, but I stayed on; Mr. Farr said nothing. I pretended to be busy scribbling words and caricaturing with no likeness Mr. Solomon's toucan profile and the snub copy-boy who whistled out of tune behind the windows of the telephone box. I wrote my name, 'Reporters' Room, *Tawe News*, Tawe, South Wales, England, Europe, The Earth.' And a list of books I had not written: 'Land of My Fathers, a Study of the Welsh Character in all its aspects'; 'Eighteen, a Provincial Autobiography.'; 'The Merciless Ladies, a Novel.' Still Mr. Farr did not look up. I wrote 'Hamlet.' Surely Mr. Farr, stubbornly transcribing his council notes had not forgotten. I heard Mr. Solomon mutter, leaning over his shoulder: 'To aitch with Alderman Daniels.' Half-past one. Ted was in a dream. I spent a long time putting on my overcoat, tied my Old Grammarian's scarf one way and then another.

'Some people are too lazy to take their half-days off,' said Mr. Farr suddenly. 'Six o'clock in the "Lamps" back bar.' He did not turn round or stop writing.

'Going for a nice walk?' asked my mother.

'Yes, on the common. Don't keep tea waiting.'

I went to the Plaza. 'Press,' I said to the girl with the Tyrolean hat and skirt.

'There's been two reporters this week.'

'Special notice.'

She showed me to a seat. During the educational film, with the rude seeds hugging and sprouting in front of my eyes and plants like arms and legs, I thought of the bob women and the pansy sailors in the dives. There might be a quarrel with razors, and once Ted Williams found a lip outside the Mission to Seamen. It had a small moustache. The sinuous plants danced on the screen. If only Tawe were a larger sea-town, there would be curtained rooms underground with blue films. The potato's life came to an end. Then I entered an American college and danced with the president's daughter. The hero, called Lincoln, tall and dark with good teeth, I displaced quickly, and the girl spoke my name as she held his shadow, the singing college chorus in sailors' hats and bathing dresses called me big boy and king, Jack Oakie and I sped up the field, and on the shoulders of the crowd the president's daughter and I brought across the shifting-coloured curtain with a kiss that left me giddy and bright-eyed as I walked out of the cinema into the strong lamplight and the new rain.

A whole wet hour to waste in the crowds. I watched the queue outside the Empire and studied the posters of *Nuit de Paris*, and thought of the long legs and startling faces of the chorus girls I had seen walking arm in arm, earlier that week, up and down the streets in the winter sunshine, their mouths, I remembered remarking and treasuring for the first page of 'The Merciless Ladies' that was never begun, like crimson scars, their hair raven-black or silver; their scent and paint reminded me of the hot and chocolate-coloured East, their eyes were pools. Lola de Kenway, Babs Courcey, Ramona Day would be with me all my life. Until I died, of a wasting, painless disease, and spoke my prepared last words, they would always walk with me, recalling me to my dead youth in the vanished High Street nights when the shop windows were blazing, and singing came out of the pubs, and sirens from the Hafod sat in the steaming chip shops with their handbags on their knees and their ear-rings rattling. I stopped to look at the window of Dirty Black's, the Fancy Man, but it was innocent; there were only itching and sneezing powders, stink bombs, rubber pens, and Charlie masks; all the novelties were inside, but I dared not go in for fear a woman should serve me, Mrs. Dirty Black with a moustache and knowing eyes, or a thin, dog-faced girl I saw there once, who winked and smelt of seaweed. In the market I bought pink cachous. You never knew.

The back room of 'The Three Lamps' was full of elderly men. Mr. Farr had not arrived. I leant against the bar, between an alderman and a solicitor, drinking bitter, wishing that my father could see me now and glad, at the same time, that he was visiting Uncle A. in Aberavon. He could not fail to see that I was a boy no longer, nor fail to be angry at the angle of my fag and my hat and the threat of the clutched tankard. I liked the taste of beer, its live, white lather, its brass-bright depths, the sudden world through the wet brown walls of the glass, the tilted rush to the lips and the slow swallowing down to the lapping belly, the salt on the tongue, the foam at the corners.

'Same again, miss.' She was middle-aged. 'One for you, miss?'

'Not during hours, ta all the same.'

'You're welcome.'

Was that an invitation to drink with her afterwards, to wait at the back door until she glided out, and then to walk through the night, along the promenade and sands, on to a soft dune where couples lay loving under their coats and looking at the Mumbles lighthouse? She was plump and plain, her netted hair was auburn and wisped with grey. She gave me my change like a mother giving her boy pennies for the pictures, and I would not go out with her if she put cream on it.

Mr. Farr hurried down High Street, savagely refusing laces and matches, averting his eyes from the shabby crowds. He knew that the poor and the sick and the ugly, unwanted people were so close around him that, with one look of recognition, one gesture of sympathy, he would be lost among them and the evening would be spoiled for ever.

'You're a pint man then,' he said at my elbow.

'Good evening, Mr. Farr. Only now and then for a change. What's yours? Dirty night,' I said.

Safe in a prosperous house, out of the way of the rain and the unsettling streets, where the poor and the past could not touch him, he took his glass lazily in the company of business and professional men and raised it to the light. 'It's going to get dirtier,' he said. 'You wait till the "Fishguard." Here's health! You can see the sailors knitting there. And the old fish-girls in the "Jersey." Got to go to the w. for a breath of fresh air.'

Mr. Evans the Produce came in quickly through a side door hidden by curtains, whispered his drink, shielded it with his overcoat, swallowed it in secrecy.

'Similar,' said Mr. Farr, 'and half for his nibs.'

The bar was too high class to look like Christmas. A notice said 'No Ladies.'

We left Mr. Evans gulping in his tent.

Children screamed in Goat Street, and one boy, out of season, pulled my sleeve, crying: 'Penny for the guy!' Big women in men's caps barricaded their doorways, and a posh girl gave us the wink at the corner of the green iron convenience opposite the Carlton Hotel. We entered to music, the bar was hung with ribbons and balloons, a tubercular tenor clung to the piano, behind the counter Leslie Bird's pretty barmaid was twitting a group of young men who leant far over and asked to see her garters and invited her to gins and limes and lonely midnight walks and moist adventures in the cinema. Mr. Farr sneered down his glass as I watched the young men enviously and saw how much she liked their ways, how she slapped their hands lightly and wriggled back, in pride of her prettiness and gaiety, to pull the beer-handles.

'Toop little Twms from the Valleys. There'll be some puking to-night,' he said with pleasure.

Other young men, sleek-haired, pale, and stocky, with high cheek-bones and deep eyes, bright ties, double-breasted waistcoats and wide trousers, some pocked from the pits, their broad hands scarred and damaged, all exultantly half-drunk, stood singing round the piano, and the tenor with the fallen chest led in a clear voice. Oh! to be able to join in the suggestive play or the rocking choir, to shout *Bread of Heaven*, with my shoulders back and my arms linked with Little Moscow, or to be called 'saucy' and 'a one' as I joked and ogled at the counter, making innocent, dirty love that could come to nothing among the spilt beer and piling glasses.

'Let's get away from the bloody nightingales,' said Mr. Farr.

'Too much bloody row,' I said.

'Now we're coming to somewhere.' We crawled down Strand alleys by the side of the mortuary, through a gas-lit lane where hidden babies cried together and reached the 'Fishguard' door as a man, muffled like Mr. Evans, slid out in front of us with a bottle or a black-jack in one gloved hand. The bar was empty. An old man whose hands trembled sat behind the counter, staring at his turnip watch.

'Merry Christmas, Pa.'

'Good evening, Mr. F.'

'Drop of rum, Pa.'

A red bottle shook over two glasses.

'Very special poison, son.'

'This'll make your eyes bulge,' said Mr. Farr.

My iron head stood high and firm, no sailors' rum could rot the rock of my belly. Poor Leslie Bird the port-sipper, and little Gil Morris who marked dissipation under his eyes with a blacklead every Saturday night, I wished they could have seen me now, in the dark, stunted room with photographs of boxers peeling on the wall.

'More poison, Pa,' I said.

'Where's the company tonight? gone to the Riviera?'

'They're in the snuggery, Mr. F., there's a party for Mrs. Prothero's daughter.'

In the back room, under a damp royal family, a row of black-dressed women on a hard bench sat laughing and crying, short glasses lined by their Guinnesses. On an opposite bench two men in jerseys drank appreciatively, nodding at the emotions of the women. And on the one chair, in the middle of the room, an old woman, with a bonnet tied under her chins, a feather boa, and white gym-shoes, tittered and wept above the rest. We sat on the men's bench. One of the two touched his cap with a sore hand.

'What's the party, Jack?' asked Mr. Farr. 'Meet my colleague, Mr. Thomas; this is Jack Stiff, the mortuary keeper.'

Jack Stiff spoke from the side of his mouth. 'It's Mrs. Prothero there. We call her Old Garbo because she isn't like her, see. She had a message from the hospital about an hour ago, Mrs. Harris's Winifred brought it here, to say her second daughter's died in pod.'

'Baby girl dead, too,' said the man at his side.

'So all the old girls came round to sympathize, and they made a big collection for her, and now she's beginning to drink it up and treating round. We've had a couple of pints from her already.'

'Shameful!'

The rum burned and kicked in the hot room, but my head felt tough as a hill and I could write twelve books before morning and roll the 'Carlton' barmaid, like a barrel, the length of Tawe sands.

'Drinks for the troops!'

Before a new audience, the women cried louder, patting Mrs. Prothero's knees and hands, adjusting her bonnet, praising her dead daughter.

'What'll you have, Mrs. Prothero, dear?'

'No, have it with me, dear, best in the house.'

'Well, a Guinness tickles my fancy.'

'And a little something in it, dear.'

'Just for Margie's sake, then.'

'Think if she was here now, dear, singing *One of the Ruins* or *Cockles and Mussels*; she had a proper madam's voice.'

'Oh, don't, Mrs. Harris!'

'There, we're only bucking you up. Grief killed the cat, Mrs. Prothero. Let's have a song together, dear.'

'The pale moon was rising above the grey mountain,
The sun was declining beneath the blue sea,
When I strolled with my love to the pure crystal fountain,'

Mrs. Prothero sang.

'It was her daughter's favourite song,' said Jack Stiff's friend.

Mr. Farr tapped me on the shoulder; his hand fell slowly from a great height and his thin, bird's voice spoke from a whirring circle on the ceiling. 'A drop of out-of-doors for you and me.' The gamps and bonnets, the white gym-shoes, the bottles and the mildew king, the singing mortuary man, the *Rose of Tralee*, swam together in the snuggery; two small men, Mr. Farr and his twin brother, led me on an ice-rink to the door, and the night air slapped me down. The evening happened suddenly. A wall slumped over and knocked off my trilby; Mr. Farr's brother disappeared under the cobbles. Here came a wall like a buffalo; dodge him, son. Have a drop of angostura, have a drop of brandy, Fernet Branca, Polly, Ooo! the mother's darling! have a hair of the dog.

'Feeling better now?'

I sat in a plush chair I had never seen before, sipping a mothball drink and appreciating an argument between Ted Williams and Mr. Farr. Mr. Farr was saying sternly: 'You came in here to look for sailors.'

'No, I didn't then,' said Ted. 'I came for local colour.'

The notices on the walls were: '"The Lord Jersey." Prop.: Titch Thomas.' 'No Betting.' 'No Swearing, B——you.' 'The Lord helps Himself, but you mustn't.' 'No Ladies allowed, except Ladies.'

'This is a funny pub,' I said. 'See the notices?'

'Okay now?'

'I'm feeling upsydaisy.'

'There's a pretty girl for you. Look, she's giving you the glad.'

'But she's got no nose.'

My drink, like winking, had turned itself into beer. A hammer tapped. 'Order! order!' At a sound in a new saloon a collarless chairman with a cigar called on Mr. Jenkins to provide *The Lily of Laguna*.

'By request,' said Mr. Jenkins.

'Order! order! for Katie Sebastopol Street. What is it, Katie?'

She sang the National Anthem.

'Mr. Fred Jones will supply his usual dirty one.'

A broken baritone voice spoiled the chorus: I recognised it as my own, and drowned it.

A girl of the Salvation Army avoided the arms of two firemen and sold them a *War Cry*.

A young man with a dazzling handkerchief round his head, black and white holiday shoes with holes for the toes, and no socks, danced until the bar cried: 'Mabel!'

Ted clapped at my side. 'That's style! "Nijinsky of the Night-world," there's a story! Wonder if I can get an interview?'

'Half a crack,' said Mr. Farr.

'Don't make me cross.'

A wind from the docks tore up the street, I heard the rowdy dredger in the bay and a boat blowing to come in, the gas-lamps bowed and bent, then again smoke closed about the stained walls with George and Mary dripping above the women's bench, and Jack Stiff whispered, holding his hand in front of him like the paw of an animal: 'Old Garbo's gone.'

The sad and jolly women huddled together.

'Mrs. Harris's little girl got the message wrong. Old Garbo's daughter's right as rain, the baby was born dead. Now the old girls want their money back, but they can't find Garbo anywhere.' He licked his hand. 'I know where she's gone.'

His friend said: 'To a boozer over the bridge.'

In low voices the women reviled Mrs. Prothero, liar, adulteress, mother of bastards, thief.

'She got you know what.'

'Never cured it.'

'Got Charlie tattooed on her.'

'Three and eight she owes me.'

'Two and ten.'

'Money for my teeth.'

'One and a tanner out of my Old Age.'

Who kept filling my glass? Beer ran down my cheek and my collar. My mouth was full of saliva. The bench spun. The cabin of the 'Fishguard' tilted. Mr. Farr retreated slowly; the telescope twisted, and his face, with wide and hairy nostrils, breathed against mine.

'Mr. Thomas is going to get sick.'

'Mind your brolly, Mrs. Arthur.'

'Take his head.'

The last tram clanked home. I did not have the penny for the fare. 'You get off here. Careful!' The revolving hill to my father's house reached to the sky. Nobody was up. I crept to a wild bed, and the wallpaper lakes converged and sucked me down.

Sunday was a quiet day, though St. Mary's bells, a mile away, rang on, long after church time, in the holes of my head. Knowing that I would never drink again, I lay in bed until midday dinner and remembered the unsteady shapes and far-off voices of the ten o'clock town. I read the newspapers. All news was bad that morning, but an article called 'Our Lord was a Flower-lover' moved me to tears of bewilderment and contrition. I excused myself from the Sunday joint and three vegetables.

In the park in the afternoon I sat alone near the deserted bandstand. I caught a ball of waste paper that the wind blew down the gravel path towards the rockery, and, straightening it out and holding it on my knee, wrote the first three lines of a poem without hope. A dog nosed me out where I crouched, behind a bare tree in the cold, and rubbed its nose against my hand. 'My only friend,' I said. It stayed with me up to the early dusk, sniffing and scratching.

On Monday morning, with shame and hate, afraid to look at them again, I destroyed the article and the poem, throwing the pieces on to the top of the wardrobe, and I told Leslie Bird in the tram to the office: 'You should have been with us, Saturday, Christ!'

Early on Tuesday night, which was Christmas Eve, I walked, with a borrowed half-crown, into the back room of the 'Fishguard.' Jack Stiff was alone. The women's bench was covered with sheets of newspaper. A bunch of balloons hung from the lamp.

'Here's health!'

'Merry Christmas!'

'Where's Mrs. Prothero?'

His hand was bandaged now. 'Oh! You haven't heard? She spent all the collection money. She took it over the bridge to the "Heart's Delight." She didn't let one of the old girls see her. It was over a pound. She'd spent a lot of it before they found her daughter wasn't dead. She couldn't face them then. Have this one with me. So she finished it up by stop-tap Monday. Then a couple of men from the banana boats saw her walking across the bridge, and she stopped half-way. But they weren't in time.'

'Merry Christmas!'

'We got a pair of gym-shoes on our slab.'

None of Old Garbo's friends came in that night.

When I showed this story a long time later to Mr. Farr, he said: 'You got it all wrong. You got the people mixed. The boy with the handkerchief danced in the "Jersey." Fred Jones was singing in the "Fishguard." Never mind. Come and have one to-night in the "Nelson." There's a girl down there who'll show you where the sailor bit her. And there's a policeman who knew Jack Johnson.

'I'll put them all in a story by and by,' I said.

One Warm Saturday

The young man in a sailor's jersey, sitting near the summer huts to see the brown and white women coming out and the groups of pretty-faced girls with pale vees and scorched backs who picked their way delicately on ugly, red-toed feet over the sharp stones to the sea, drew on the sand a large, indented woman's figure; and a naked child, just out of the sea, ran over it and shook water, marking on the figure two wide wet eyes and a hole in the footprinted middle. He rubbed the woman away and drew a paunched man; the child ran over it, tossing her hair, and shook a row of buttons down its belly and a line of drops, like piddle in a child's drawing, between the long legs stuck with shells.

In a huddle of picnicking women and their children, stretched out limp and damp in the sweltering sun or fussing over paper carriers or building castles that were at once destroyed by the tattered march of other picnickers to different pieces of the beach, among the ice-cream cries, the angrily happy shouts of boys playing ball, and the screams of girls as the sea rose to their waists, the young man sat alone with the shadows of his failure at his side. Some silent husbands, with rolled up trousers and suspenders dangling, paddled slowly on the border of the sea, paddling women, in thick, black picnic dresses, laughed at their own legs, dogs chased stones, and one proud boy rode the water on a rubber seal. The young man, in his wilderness, saw the holiday Saturday set down before him, false and pretty, as a flat picture under the vulgar sun; the disporting families with paper bags, buckets and spades, parasols and bottles, the happy, hot, and aching girls with sunburn liniments in their bags, the bronzed young men with chests, and the envious, white young men in waistcoats, the thin, pale, hairy, pathetic legs of the husbands silently walking through the water, the plump and curly, shaven-headed and bowed-backed children up to no sense with unrepeatable delight in the dirty sand, moved him, he thought dramatically in his isolation, to an old shame and pity; outside all holiday, like a young man doomed for ever to the company of his maggots, beyond the high and ordinary, sweating, sun-awakened power and stupidity of the summer flesh on a day and a world out, he caught the ball that a small boy had whacked into the air with a tin tray, and rose to throw it back.

The boy invited him to play. A friendly family stood waiting some way off, the tousled women with their dresses tucked in their knickers, the bare-footed men in shirt-sleeves, a number of children in slips and cut-down underwear. He bowled bitterly to a father standing with a tray before the wicket of hats. 'The lone wolf playing ball,' he said to himself as the tray whirled. Chasing the ball towards the sea, passing undressing women with a rush and a wink, tripping over a castle into a coil of wet girls lying like snakes, soaking his shoes as he grabbed the ball off a wave, he felt his happiness return in a boast of the body, and, 'Look out, Duckworth, here's a fast one coming,' he cried to the mother behind the hats. The ball bounced on a boy's head. In and out of the scattered families, among the sandwiches and clothes, uncles and mothers fielded the bouncing ball. A bald man, with his shirt hanging out, returned it in the wrong direction, and a collie carried it into the sea. Now it was mother's turn with the tray. Tray and ball together flew over her head. An uncle in a panama smacked the ball to the dog, who swam with it out of reach. They offered the young man egg-and-cress sandwiches and warm stout, and he and an uncle and a father sat down on the *Evening Post* until the sea touched their feet.

Alone again, hot and unhappy, for the boasting minute when he ran among the unknown people lying and running loudly at peace was struck away, like a ball, he said, into the sea, he walked to a space on the beach where a hell-fire preacher on a box marked 'Mr. Matthews' was talking to a congregation of expressionless women. Boys with pea-shooters sat quietly near him. A ragged man collected nothing in a cap. Mr. Matthews shook his cold hands, stormed at the holiday, and cursed the summer from his shivering box. He cried for a new warmth. The strong sun shone into his bones, and he buttoned his coat collar. Valley children, with sunken, impudent eyes, quick tongues and singing voices, chest thin as shells, gathered round the Punch and Judy and the Stop Me tricycles, and he denied them all. He contradicted the girls in their underclothes combing and powdering, and the modest girls cleverly dressing under tents of towels.

As Mr. Matthews cast down the scarlet town, drove out the bare-bellied boys who danced around the ice-cream man, and wound the girls' sunburnt thighs about with his black overcoat—'Down! down!' he cried, 'the night is upon us'—the young man in dejection stood, with a shadow at his shoulder, and thought of Porthcawl's Coney Beach, where his friends were rocking with girls on the Giant Racer or tearing in the Ghost Train down the skeletons' tunnel. Leslie Bird would have his arms full of coconuts. Brenda was with Herbert at the rifle-range. Gil Morris was buying Molly a cocktail with a cherry at the 'Esplanade.' Here he stood, listening to Mr. Matthews, the retired drinker, crying darkness on the evening sands, with money hot in his pocket and Saturday burning away.

In his loneliness he had refused their invitations. Herbert, in his low, red sports car, G.B. at the back, a sea-blown nymph on the radiator, called at his father's house, but he said: 'I'm not in the mood, old man. I'm going to spend a quiet day. Enjoy yourselves. Don't take too much pop.' Only waiting for the sun to set, he stood in the sad circle with the pleasureless women who were staring at a point in the sky behind their prophet, and wished the morning back. Oh, boy! to be wasting his money now on the rings and ranges of the fair, to be sitting in the chromium lounge with a short worth one and six and a Turkish cigarette, telling the latest one to the girls, seeing the sun, through the palms in the lounge window, sink over the promenade, over the Bath chairs, the cripples and widows, the beach-trousered, kerchiefed, week-end wives, the smart, kiss-curled girls with plain and spectacled girl friends, the innocent, swaggering, loud bad boys, and the poms at the ankles, and the cycling sweet-men. Ronald had sailed to Ilfracombe on the *Lady Moira*, and, in the thick saloon, with a party from Brynhyfryd, he'd be knocking back nips without a thought that on the sands at home his friend was alone and pussyfoot at six o'clock, and the evening dull as a chapel. All his friends had vanished into their pleasures.

He thought: Poets live and walk with their poems; a man with visions needs no other company; Saturday is a crude day; I must go home and sit in my bedroom by the boiler. But he was not a poet living and walking, he was a young man in a sea town on a warm bank holiday, with two pounds to spend; he had no visions, only two pounds and a small body with its feet on the littered sand; serenity was for old men; and he moved away, over the railway points, on to the tramlined road.

He snarled at the flower clock in Victoria Gardens.

'And what shall a prig do now?' he said aloud, causing a young woman on a bench opposite the white-tiled urinal to smile and put her novel down.

She had chestnut hair arranged high on her head in an old-fashioned way, in loose coils and a bun, and a Woolworth's white rose grew out of it and drooped to touch her ear. She wore a white frock with a red paper flower pinned on the breast, and rings and bracelets that came from a fun-fair stall. Her eyes were small and quite green.

He marked, carefully and coldly in one glance, all the unusual details of her appearance; it was the calm, unstartled certainty of her bearing before his glance from head to foot, the innocent knowledge, in her smile and the set of her head, that she was defended by her gentleness and accessible strangeness against all rude encounters and picking looks, that made his fingers tremble. Though her frock was long and the collar high, she could as well be naked there on the blistered bench. Her smile confessed her body bare and spotless and willing and warm under the cotton, and she waited without guilt.

How beautiful she is, he thought, with his mind on words and his eyes on her hair and red and white skin, how beautifully she waits for me, though she does not know she is waiting and I can never tell her.

He had stopped and was staring. Like a confident girl before a camera, she sat smiling, her hands folded, her head slightly to one side so that the rose brushed her neck. She accepted his admiration. The girl in a million took his long look to herself, and cherished his stupid love.

Midges flew into his mouth. He hurried on shamefully. At the gates of the gardens he turned to see her for the last time on earth. She had lost her calm with his abrupt and awkward going, and stared in confusion after him. One hand was raised as though to beckon him back. If he waited, she would call him. He walked round the corner and heard her voice, a hundred voices, and all hers, calling his name, and a hundred names that were all his, over the bushy walls.

And what shall the terrified prig of a love-mad young man do next? he asked his reflection silently in the distorting mirror of the empty 'Victoria' saloon. His ape-like hanging face, with 'Bass' across the forehead, gave back a cracked sneer.

If Venus came in on a plate, said the two red, melon-slice lips, I would ask for vinegar to put on her.

She could drive my guilt out; she could smooth away my shame; why didn't I stop to talk to her? he asked.

You saw a queer tart in a park, his reflection answered, she was a child of nature, oh my! oh my! Did you see the dewdrops in her hair? Stop talking to the mirror like a man in a magazine, I know you too well.

A new head, swollen and lop-jawed, wagged behind his shoulder. He spun round to hear the barman say:

'Has the one and only let you down? You look like death warmed up. Have this one on the house. Free beer to-day. Free X's.' He pulled the beer handle. 'Only the best served here. Straight from the rust. You do look queer,' he said, 'the only one saved from the wreck and the only wreck saved. Here's looking at you!' He drank the beer he had drawn.

'May I have a glass of beer, please?'

'What do you think this is, a public house?'

On the polished table in the middle of the saloon the young man drew, with a finger dipped in strong, the round head of a girl and piled a yellow froth of hair upon it.

'Ah! dirty, dirty!' said the barman, running round from behind the counter and rubbing the head away with a dry cloth.

Shielding the dirtiness with his hat, the young man wrote his name on the edge of the table and watched the letters dry and fade.

Through the open bay-window, across the useless railway covered with sand, he saw the black dots of bathers, the stunted huts, the jumping dwarfs round the Punch and Judy, and the tiny religious circle. Since he had walked and played down there in the crowded wilderness excusing his despair, searching for company though he refused it, he had found his own true happiness and lost her all in one bewildering and clumsy half a minute by the 'Gentlemen' and the flower clock. Older and wiser and no better, he would have looked in the mirror to see if his discovery and loss had marked themselves upon his face in shadows under the eyes or lines about the mouth, were it not for the answer he knew he would receive from the distorted reflection.

The barman came to sit near him, and said in a false voice: 'Now you tell me all about it, I'm a regular storehouse of secrets.'

'There isn't anything to tell. I saw a girl in Victoria Gardens and I was too shy to speak to her. She was a piece of God help us all right.'

Ashamed of his wish to be companionable, even in the depth of love and distress, with her calm face before his eyes and her smile reproving and forgiving him as he spoke, the young man defiled his girl on the bench, dragged her down into the spit and sawdust and dolled her up to make the barman say:

'I like them big myself. Once round Bessy, once round the gasworks. I missed the chance of a lifetime, too. Fifty lovelies in the nude and I'd left my Bunsen burner home.'

'Give me the same, please.'

'You mean similar.'

The barman drew a glass of beer, drank it, and drew another.

'I always have one with the customers,' he said, 'it puts us on even terms. Now we're just two heart-broken bachelors together.' He sat down again.

'You can't tell me anything I don't know,' he said. 'I've seen over twenty chorines from the Empire in this bar, drunk as printers. Oh, les girls! les limbs!'

'Will they be in to-night?'

'There's only a fellow sawing a woman in half this week.'

'Keep a half for me.'

A drunk man walked in on an invisible white line, and the barman, reeling in sympathy across the room, served him with a pint. 'Free beer to-day,' he said. 'Free X's. You've been out in the sun.'

'I've been out in the sun all day,' said the man.

'I thought you looked sunburnt.'

'That's drink,' said the man. 'I've been drinking.'

'The holiday is drawing to an end,' the young man whispered into his glass. Bye-bye blackbird, the moment is lost, he thought, examining, with an interest he could not forgive, the comic coloured postcards of mountain-buttocked women on the beach and hen-pecked, pin-legged men with telescopes, pasted on the wall beneath the picture of a terrier drinking stout; and now, with a jolly barman and a drunk in a crushed cap, he was mopping the failing day down. He tipped his hat over his forehead, and a lock of hair that fell below the hat tickled his eyelid. He saw, with a stranger's darting eye that missed no single subtlety of the wry grin or the faintest gesture drawing the shape of his death on the air, an unruly-haired young man who coughed into his hand in the corner of a rotting room and puffed the smoke of his doped Weight.

But as the drunk man weaved towards him on wilful feet, carrying his dignity as a man might carry a full glass around a quaking ship, as the barman behind the counter clattered and whistled and dipped to drink, he shook off the truthless, secret tragedy with a sneer and a blush, straightened his melancholy hat into a hard-brimmed trilby, dismissed the affected stranger. In the safe centre of his own identity, the familiar world about him like another flesh, he sat sad and content in the plain room of the undistinguished hotel at the sea-end of the shabby, spreading town where everything was happening. He had no need of the dark interior world when Tawe pressed in upon him and the eccentric ordinary people came bursting and crawling, with noise and colours, out of their houses, out of the graceless buildings, the factories and avenues, the shining shops and blaspheming chapels, the terminuses and the meeting-halls, the falling alleys and brick lanes, from the arches and shelters and holes behind the hoardings, out of the common, wild intelligence of the town.

At last the drunk man had reached him. 'Put your hand here,' he said, and turned about and tapped himself on the bottom.

The barman whistled and rose from his drink to see the young man touch the drunk on the seat of the trousers.

'What can you feel there?'

'Nothing.'

'That's right. Nothing. Nothing. There's nothing there to feel.'

'How can you sit down then?' asked the barman.

'I just sit down on what the doctor left,' the man said angrily. 'I had as good a bottom as you've got once. I was working underground in Dowlais, and the end of the world came down on me. Do you know what I got for losing my bottom? Four and three! Two and three ha'pence a cheek. That's cheaper than a pig.'

The girl from Victoria Gardens came into the bar with two friends: a blonde young girl almost as beautiful as she was, and a middle-aged woman dressed and made up to look young. The three of them sat at the table. The girl he loved ordered three ports and gins.

'Isn't it delicious weather?' said the middle-aged woman.

The barman said: 'Plenty of sky about.' With many bows and smiles he placed their drinks in front of them. 'I thought the princesses had gone to a better pub,' he said.

'What's a better pub without you, handsome?' said the blonde girl.

'This is the "Ritz" and the "Savoy," isn't it, *garçon* darling?' the girl from the Gardens said, and kissed her hand to him.

The young man in the window seat, still bewildered by the first sudden sight of her entering the darkening room, caught the kiss to himself and blushed. He thought to run out of the room and through the miracle-making Gardens, to rush into his house and hide his head in the bed-clothes and lie all night there, dressed and trembling, her voice in his ears, her green eyes wide awake under his closed eyelids. But only a sick boy with tossed blood would run from his proper love into a dream, lie down in a bedroom that was full of his shames, and sob against the feathery, fat breast and face on the damp pillow. He remembered his age and poems, and would not move.

'Tanks a million, Lou,' said the barman.

Her name was Lou, Louise, Louisa. She must be Spanish or French or a gipsy, but he could tell the street that her voice came from; he knew where her friends lived by the rise and fall of their sharp voices, and the name of the middle-aged woman was Mrs. Emerald Franklin. She was to be seen every night in the 'Jew's Harp,' sipping and spying and watching the clock.

'We've been listening to Matthews Hellfire on the sands. Down with this and down with that, and he used to drink a pint of biddy before his breakfast,' Mrs. Franklin said. 'Oh, there's a nerve!'

'And his eye on the fluff all the time,' said the blonde girl. 'I wouldn't trust him any further than Ramon Navarro behind the counter.'

'Whoops! I've gone up in the world. Last week I was Charley Chase,' said the barman.

Mrs. Franklin raised her empty glass in a gloved hand and shook it like a bell. 'Men are deceivers ever,' she said. 'And a drop of mother's ruin right around.'

'Especially Mr. Franklin,' said the barman.

'But there's a lot in what the preacher says, mind,' Mrs. Franklin said, 'about the carrying on. If you go for a constitutional after stop-tap along the sands you might as well be in Sodom and Gomorrah.'

The blonde girl laughed. 'Hark to Mrs. Grundy! I see her with a black man last Wednesday, round by the museum.'

'He was an Indian,' said Mrs. Franklin, 'from the university college, and I'd thank you to remember it. Every one's brothers under the skin, but there's no tarbrush in my family.'

'Oh, dear! oh, dear!' said Lou. 'Lay off it, there's loves. This is my birthday. It's a holiday. Put a bit of fun in it. Miaow! miaow! Marjorie, kiss Emerald and be friends.' She smiled and laughed at them both. She winked at the barman, who was filling their glasses to the top. 'Here's to your blue eyes, *garçon*!' She had not noticed the young man in the corner. 'And one for grand-dad there,' she said, smiling at the swaying, drunk man. 'He's twenty-one to-day. There! I've made him smile.'

The drunk man made a deep, dangerous bow, lifted his hat, stumbled against the mantelpiece, and his full pint in his free hand was steady as a rock. 'The prettiest girl in Carmarthenshire,' he said.

'This is Glamorganshire, dad,' she said, 'where's your geography? Look at him waltzing! mind your glasses! He's got that Kruschen feeling. Come on, faster! give us the Charleston.'

The drunk man, with the pint held high, danced until he fell, and all the time he never spilt a drop. He lay at Lou's feet on the dusty floor and grinned up at her in confidence and affection. 'I fell,' he said. 'I could dance like a trooper when I had a beatyem.'

'He lost his bottom at the last trump,' the barman explained.

'When did he lose his bottom?' said Mrs. Franklin.

'When Gabriel blew his whistle down in Dowlais.'

'You're pulling my leg.'

'It's a pleasure, Mrs. Em. Hoi, you! get up from the vomitorium.'

The man wagged his end like a tail, and growled at Lou's feet.

'Put your head on my foot. Be comfy. Let him lie there,' she said.

He went to sleep at once.

'I can't have drunks on the premises.

'You know where to go then.'

'Cru-el Mrs. Franklin!'

'Go on, attend to your business. Serve the young man in the corner, his tongue's hanging out.'

'Cru-el lady!'

As Mrs. Franklin called attention to the young man, Lou peered shortsightedly across the saloon and saw him sitting with his back to the window.

'I'll have to get glasses,' she said.

'You'll have plenty of glasses before the night's out.'

'No, honest, Marjorie, I didn't know anyone was there. I do beg your pardon, you in the corner,' she said.

The barman switched on the light. 'A bit of *lux in tenebris*.'

'Oh!' said Lou.

The young man dared not move for fear that he might break the long light of her scrutiny, the enchantment shining like a single line of light between them, or startle her into speaking; and he did not conceal the love in his eyes, for she could pierce through to it as easily as she could turn his heart in his chest and make it beat above the noises of the two friends' hurried conversation, the rattle of glasses behind the counter where the barman spat and polished and missed nothing, and the snores of the comfortable sleeper. Nothing can hurt me. Let the barman jeer. Giggle in your glass, our Em. I'm telling the world, I'm walking in clover, I'm staring at Lou like a fool, she's my girl, she's my lily. O love! O love! She's no lady, with her sing-song Tontine voice, she drinks like a deep-sea diver; but Lou, I'm yours, and Lou, you're mine. He refused to meditate on her calmness now and twist her beauty into words. She was nothing under the sun or moon but his. Unashamed and certain, he smiled at her; and, though he was prepared for all, her answering smile made his fingers tremble again, as they had trembled in the Gardens, and reddened his cheeks and drove his heart to a gallop.

'Harold, fill the young man's glass up,' Mrs. Franklin said.

The barman stood still, a duster in one hand and a dripping glass in the other.

'Have you got water in your ears? Fill the young man's glass!'

The barman put the duster to his eyes. He sobbed. He wiped away the mock tears.

'I thought I was attending a *première* and this was the royal box,' he said.

'He's got water on the brain, not in his earhole,' said Marjorie.

'I dreamt it was a beautiful tragi-comedy entitled "Love at First Sight, or, Another Good Man gone wrong." Act one in a boozer by the sea.'

The two women tapped their foreheads.

Lou said, still smiling: 'Where was the second act?'

Her voice was as gentle as he had imagined it to be before her gay and nervous playing with the over-familiar barman and the inferior women. He saw her as a wise, soft girl whom no hard company could spoil, for her soft self, bare to the heart, broke through every defence of her sensual falsifiers. As he thought this, phrasing her gentleness, faithlessly running to words away from the real room and his love in the middle, he woke with a start and saw her lively body six steps from him, no calm heart dressed in a sentence, but a pretty girl, to be got and kept. He must catch hold of her fast. He got up to cross to her.

'I woke before the second act came on,' said the barman. 'I'd sell my dear old mother to see that. Dim lights. Purple couches. Ecstatic bliss. Là, là chèrie!'

The young man sat down at the table, next to her.

Harold, the barman, leaned over the counter and cupped his hand to his ear.

The man on the floor rolled in his sleep, and his head lay in the spittoon.

'You should have come and sat here a long time ago,' Lou whispered. 'You should have stopped to talk to me in the Gardens. Were you shy?'

'I was too shy,' the young man whispered.

'Whispering isn't manners. I can't hear a word,' said the barman.

At a sign from the young man, a flick of the fingers that sent the waiters in evening dress bustling with oysters about the immense room, the barman filled the glasses with port, gin, and Nutbrown.

'We never drink with strangers,' Mrs. Franklin said, laughing.

'He isn't a stranger,' said Lou, 'are you Jack?'

He threw a pound note on the table: 'Take the damage.'

The evening that had been over before it began raced along among the laughter of the charming women sharp as knives, and the stories of the barman, who should be on the stage, and Lou's delighted smiles and silences at his side. Now she is safe and sure, he thought, after her walking like my doubtful walking, around the lonely distances of the holiday. In the warm, spinning middle they were close and alike. The town and the sea and the last pleasure-makers drifted into the dark that had nothing to do with them, and left this one room burning.

One by one, some lost men from the dark shuffled into the bar, drank sadly, and went out. Mrs. Franklin, flushed and dribbling waved her glass at their departures. Harold winked behind their backs. Marjorie showed them her long, white legs.

'Nobody loves us except ourselves,' said Harold. 'Shall I shut the bar and keep the riff-raff out?'

'Lou is expecting Mr. O'Brien, but don't let that stop you,' Marjorie said. 'He's her sugar daddy from old Ireland.'

'Do you love Mr. O'Brien?' the young man whispered.

'How could I, Jack?'

He could see Mr. O'Brien as a witty, tall fellow of middle age, with waved greying hair and a clipped bit of dirt on his upper lip, a flash ring on his marriage finger, a pouched knowing eye, dummy dressed with a whalebone waist, a broth of a man about Cardiff, Lou's horrible lover tearing towards her now down the airless streets in the firm's car. The young man clenched his hand on the table covered with dead, and sheltered her in the warm strength of his fist. 'My round, my round,' he said, 'up again, plenty! Doubles, trebles, Mrs. Franklin is a jibber.'

'My mother never had a jibber.'

'Oh, Lou!' he said, 'I am more than happy with you.'

'Coo! coo! hear the turtle doves.'

'Let them coo,' said Marjorie. 'I could coo, too.'

The barman looked around him in surprise. He raised his hands, palms up, and cocked his head.

'The bar is full of birds,' he said.

'Emerald's laying an egg,' he said, as Mrs. Franklin rocked in her chair.

Soon the bar was full of customers. The drunk man woke up and ran out, leaving his cap in a brown pool. Sawdust dropped from his hair. A small, old, round, red-faced, cheery man sat facing the young man and Lou, who held hands under the table and rubbed their legs against each other.

'What a night for love!' said the old man. 'On such a night as this did Jessica steal from the wealthy Jew. Do you know where that comes from?'

'*The Merchant of Venice*,' Lou said. 'But you're an Irishman, Mr. O'Brien.'

'I culd have sworn you were a tall man with a little tish,' said the young man gravely.

'What's the weapons, Mr. O'Brien?'

'Brandies at dawn, I should think, Mrs. Franklin.'

'I never described Mr. O'Brien to you at all. You're

dreaming!' Lou whispered. 'I wish this night could go on for ever.'

'But not here. Not in the bar. In a room with a big bed.'

'A bed in a bar,' said the old man, 'if you'll pardon me hearing you, that's what I've always wanted. Think of it, Mrs. Franklin.'

The barman bobbed up from behind the counter.

'Time, gentlemen and others!'

The sober strangers departed to Mrs. Franklin's laughter.

The lights went out.

'Lou, don't you lose me.'

'I've got your hand.'

'Press it hard, hurt it.'

'Break his bloody neck,' Mrs. Franklin said in the dark. 'No offence meant.'

'Marjorie smack hand,' said Marjorie. 'Let's get out of the dark. Harold's a rover in the dark.'

'And the girl guides.'

'Let's take a bottle each and go down to Lou's,' she said.

'I'll buy the bottles,' said Mr. O'Brien.

'It's you don't lose me now,' Lou whispered. 'Hold on to me, Jack. The others won't stay long. Oh, Mr. Christ, I wish it was just you and me!'

'Will it be just you and me?'

'You and me and Mr. Moon.'

Mr. O'Brien opened the saloon door. 'Pile into the Rolls, you ladies. The gentlemen are going to see to the medicine.'

The young man felt Lou's quick kiss on his mouth before she followed Marjorie and Mrs. Franklin out.

'What do you say we split the drinks?' said Mr. O'Brien.

'Look what I found in the lavatory,' said the barman, 'he was singing on the seat.' He appeared behind the counter with the drunk man leaning on his arm.

They all climbed into the car.

'First stop, Lou's.'

The young man, on Lou's knee, saw the town in a daze spin by them, the funnelled and masted smoke-blue outline of the still, droning docks, the lightning lines of the poor streets growing longer, and the winking shops that were snapped out one by one. The car smelt of scent and powder and flesh. He struck with his elbow, by accident, Mrs. Franklin's upholstered breast. Her thighs, like cushions, bore the drunk man's rolling weight. He was bumped and tossed on a lump of woman. Breasts, legs, bellies, hands, touched, warmed, and smothered him. On through the night, towards Lou's bed, towards the unbelievable end of the dying holiday, they tore past black houses and bridges, a station in a smoke cloud, and drove up a steep side street with one weak lamp in a circle of railings at the top, and swerved into a space where a tall tenement house stood surrounded by cranes, standing ladders, poles and girders, barrows, brick-heaps.

They climbed to Lou's room up many flights of dark, perilous stairs. Washing hung on the rails outside closed doors. Mrs. Franklin, fumbling alone with the drunk man behind the others, trod in a bucket, and a lucky black cat ran over her foot. Lou led the young man by the hand through a passage marked with names and doors, lit a match, and whispered: 'It won't be very long. Be good and patient with Mr. O'Brien. Here it is. Come in first. Welcome to you, Jack!' She kissed him again at the door of her room.

She turned on the lights, and he walked with her proudly into her own room, into the room that he would come to know, and saw a wide bed, a gramaphone on a chair, a wash-basin half-hidden in a corner, a gas fire and a cooking ring, a closed cupboard, and her photograph in a cardboard frame on the chest of drawers with no handles. Here she slept and ate. In the double bed she lay all night, pale and curled, sleeping on her left side. When he lived with her always, he would not allow her to dream. No other men must lie and love in her head. He spread his fingers on her pillow.

'Why do you live at the top of the Eiffel Tower!' said the barman, coming in.

'What a climb!' said Mr. O'Brien. 'But it's very nice and private when you get here.'

'If you get here!' said Mrs. Franklin. 'I'm dead beat. This old nuisance weighs a ton. Lie down, lie down on the floor and go to sleep. The old nuisance!' she said fondly. 'What's your name?'

'Ernie,' the drunk man said, raising his arm to shield his face.

'Nobody's going to bite you, Ernie. Here, give him a nip of whiskey. Careful! Don't pour it on your waistcoat; you'll be squeezing your waistcoat in the morning. Pull the curtains, Lou, I can see the wicked old moon,' she said.

'Does it put ideas in your head?'

'I love the moon,' said Lou.

'There never was a young lover who didn't love the moon.' Mr. O'Brien gave the young man a cheery smile, and patted his hand. His own hand was red and hairy. 'I could see at the flash of a glance that Lou and this nice young fellow were made for each other. I could see it in their eyes. Dear me, no! I'm not so old and blind I can't see love in front of my nose. Couldn't you see it, Mrs. Franklin? Couldn't you see it, Marjorie?'

In the long silence, Lou collected glasses from the cupboard as though she had not heard Mr. O'Brien speak. She drew the curtains, shut out the moon, sat on the edge of her bed with her feet tucked under her, looked at her photograph as at a stranger, folded her hands as she folded them, on the first meeting, before the young man's worship in the Gardens.

'A host of angels must be passing by,' said Mr. O'Brien. 'What a silence there is! Have I said anything out of place? Drink and be merry, to-morrow we die. What do you think I bought these lovely shining bottles for?'

The bottles were opened. The dead were lined on the mantelpiece. The whisky went down. Harold the barman and Marjorie, her dress lifted, sat in the one arm-chair together. Mrs. Franklin, with Ernie's head on her lap, sang in a sweet, trained contralto voice *The Shepherd's Lass*. Mr. O'Brien kept rhythm with his foot.

I want Lou in my arms, the young man said to himself, watching Mr. O'Brien tap and smile and the barman draw Marjorie down deep. Mrs. Franklin's voice sang sweetly in the small bedroom where he and Lou should be lying in the white bed without any smiling company to see them drown. He and Lou could go down together, one cool body weighted with a boiling stone, on to the falling, blank white, entirely empty sea, and never rise. Sitting on their bridal bed, near enough to hear his breath, she was farther from him than before they met. Then he had everything but her body; now she had given him two kisses, and everything had vanished but that beginning. He must be good and patient with Mr. O'Brien. He could wipe away the embracing, old smile with the iron back of his hand. Sink lower, lower, Harold and Marjorie, tumble like whales at Mr. O'Brien's feet.

He wished that the light would fail. In the darkness he and Lou could creep beneath the clothes and imitate the dead. Who would look for them there, if they were dead still and soundless? The others would shout to them down the dizzy stairs or rummage in

the silence about the narrow, obstacled corridors or stumble out
into the night to search for them among the cranes and ladders in
the desolation of the destroyed houses. He could hear, in the
made-up dark, Mr. O'Brien's voice cry, 'Lou, where are you?
Answer! answer!' the hollow answer of the echo, 'answer!' and
hear her lips in the cool pit of the bed secretly move around
another name and feel them move.

'A fine piece of singing, Emerald, and very naughty words.
That was a shepherd, that was,' Mr. O'Brien said.

Ernie, on the floor, began to sing in a thick, sulking voice, but
Mrs. Franklin placed her hand over his mouth and he sucked and
nuzzled it.

'What about this young shepherd?' said Mr. O'Brien, pointing
his glass at the young man. 'Can he sing as well as make love? You
ask him kindly, girlie,' he said to Lou, 'and he'll give us a song like
a nightingale.'

'Can you sing, Jack?'

'Like a crow, Lou.'

'Can't he even talk poetry? What a young man to have who
can't spout the poets to his lady!' Mr. O'Brien said.

From the cupboard Lou brought out a red-bound book and
gave it to the young man, saying: 'Can you read us a piece out of
here? The second volume's in the hatbox. Read us a dreamy piece,
Jack. It's nearly midnight.'

'Only a love poem, no other kind,' said Mr. O'Brien. 'I won't
hear anything but a love poem.'

'Soft and sweet,' Mrs. Franklin said. She took her hand away
from Ernie's mouth and looked at the ceiling.

The young man read, but not aloud, lingering on her name,
the inscription on the fly-leaf of the first volume of the collected
poems of Tennyson: 'To Louisa, from her Sunday School teacher,
Miss Gwyneth Forbes. God's in His Heaven, all's right with the
world.'

'Make it a love poem, don't forget.'

The young man read aloud, closing one eye to steady the
dancing print, *Come into the Garden, Maud*. And when he reached
the beginning of the fourth verse his voice grew louder:

> 'I said to the lily, "There is but one
> With whom she has heart to be gay.
> When will the dancers leave her alone?
> She is weary of dance and play."

Now half to the setting moon are gone,
And half to the rising day;
Low on the sand and loud on the stone
The last wheel echoes away.

'I said to the rose, "The brief night goes
In babble and revel and wine.
O young lord-lover, what sighs are those,
For one that will never be thine?
But mine, but mine," so I sware to the
    rose,
"For ever and ever, mine."'

At the end of the poem, Harold said, suddenly, his head hanging over the arm of the chair, his hair made wild, and his mouth red with lipstick: 'My grandfather remembers seeing Lord Tennyson, he was a little man with a hump.'

'No,' said the young man, 'he was tall and he had long hair and a beard.'

'Did you ever see him?'

'I wasn't born then.'

'My grandfather saw him. He had a hump.'

'Not Alfred Tennyson.'

'Lord Alfred Tennyson was a little man with a hump.'

'It couldn't have been the same Tennyson.'

'You've got the wrong Tennyson, this was the famous poet with a hump.'

Lou, on the wonderful bed, waiting for him alone of all the men, ugly or handsome, old or young, in the wide town and the small world that would be bound to fall, lowered her head and kissed her hand to him and held her hand in the river of light on the counterpane. The hand, to him, became transparent, and the light on the counterpane glowed up steadily through it in the thin shape of her palm and fingers.

'Ask Mr. O'Brien what Lord Tennyson was like,' said Mrs. Franklin. 'We appeal to you, Mr. O'Brien, did he have a hump or not?'

Nobody but the young man, for whom she lived and waited now, noticed Lou's little loving movements. She put her glowing hand to her left breast. She made a sign of secrecy on her lips.

'It depends,' Mr. O'Brien said.

The young man closed one eye again, for the bed was pitching like a ship; a sickening, hot storm out of a cigarette cloud unsettled cupboard and chest. The motions of the sea-going bedroom were calmed with the cunning closing of his eye, but he longed for night air. On sailor's legs he walked to the door.

'You'll find the House of Commons on the second floor at the end of the passage,' said Mr. O'Brien.

At the door, he turned to Lou and smiled with all his love, declaring it to the faces of the company and making her, before Mr. O'Brien's envious regard, smile back and say: 'Don't be long, Jack, Please! You mustn't be long.'

Now every one knew. Love had grown up in an evening.

'One minute, my darling,' he said. 'I'll be here.'

The door closed behind him. He walked into the wall of the passage. He lit a match. He had three left. Down the stairs, clinging to the sticky, shaking rails, rocking on see-saw floorboards, bruising his shin on a bucket, past the noises of secret lives behind doors he slid and stumbled and swore and heard Lou's voice in a fresh fever drive him on, call him to return, speak to him with such passion and abandonment that even in the darkness and the pain of his haste he was dazzled and struck still. She spoke, there on the rotting stairs in the middle of the poor house, a frightening rush of love words; from her mouth, at his ear, endearments were burned out. Hurry! hurry! Every moment is being killed. Love, adored, dear, run back and whistle to me, open the door, shout my name, lay me down. Mr. O'Brien has his hands on my side.

He ran into a cavern. A draught blew out his matches. He lurched into a room where two figures on a black heap on the floor lay whispering, and ran from there in a panic. He made water at the dead end of the passage and hurried back towards Lou's room, finding himself at last on a silent patch of stairway at the top of the house; he put out his hand, but the rail was broken and nothing there prevented a long drop to the ground down a twisted shaft that would echo and double his cry, bring out from their holes in the wall the sleeping or stirring families, the whispering figures, the blind startled turners of night into day. Lost in a tunnel near the roof, he fingered the damp walls for a door; he found a handle and gripped it hard, but it came off in his hand. Lou had led him down a longer passage than this. He remembered the number of doors: there were three on each side. He ran down the broken-railed flight into another passage and dragged his hand along the wall. Three doors, he counted. He opened the third door, walked into darkness, and groped for the switch on the left. He saw, in the sudden light, a bed and a cupboard and a chest of drawers with no handles, a gas fire, a wash-basin in the corner. No bottles. No glasses. No photograph of Lou. The red counterpane on the bed was smooth. He could not remember the colour of Lou's counterpane.

He left the light burning and opened the second door, but a strange woman's voice cried, half-asleep: 'Who is there? Is it you, Tom? Tom, put the light on.' He looked for a line of light at the foot of the next door, and stopped to listen for voices. The woman was still calling in the second room.

'Lou, where are you?' he cried. 'Answer! answer!'

'Lou, what Lou? There's no Lou here,' said a man's voice through the open door of the first dark room at the entrance to the passage.

He scampered down another flight and counted four doors with his scratched hand. One door opened and a woman in a nightdress put out her head. A child's head appeared below her.

'Where does Lou live? Do you know where Lou lives?'

The woman and the child stared without speaking.

'Lou! Lou! her name is Lou!' he heard himself shout. 'She lives here, in this house! Do you know where she lives?'

The woman caught the child by the hair and pulled her into the room. He clung to the edge of her door. The woman thrust her arm round the edge and brought down a bunch of keys sharply on his hands. The door slammed.

A young woman with a baby in a shawl stood at an open door on the opposite side of the passage, and caught his sleeve as he ran by. 'Lou who? You woke my baby.'

'I don't know her other name. She's with Mrs. Franklin and Mr. O'Brien.'

'You woke my baby.'

'Come in and find her in the bed,' a voice said from the darkness behind the young woman.

'He's woken my baby.'

He ran down the passage, holding his wet hand to his mouth. He fell against the rails of the last flight of stairs. He heard Lou's voice in his head once more whisper to him to return as the ground floor rose, like a lift full of dead, towards the rails. Hurry! hurry! I can't, I won't wait, the bridal night is being killed.

Up the rotten, bruising, mountainous stairs he climbed, in his sickness, to the passage where he had left the one light burning in an end room. The light was out. He tapped all the doors and whispered her name. He beat on the doors and shouted, and a woman, dressed in a vest and a hat, drove him out of the passage with a walking-stick.

For a long time he waited on the stairs, though there was no love now to wait for and no bed but his own too many miles away to lie in, and only the approaching day to remember his discovery. All around him the disturbed inhabitants of the house were falling back into sleep. Then he walked out of the house on to the waste space and under the leaning cranes and ladders. The light of the one weak lamp in a rusty circle fell across the brick-heaps and the broken wood and the dust that had been houses once, where the small and hardly known and never-to-be-forgotten people of the dirty town had lived and loved and died and, always, lost.

Plenty of Furniture

1

Every inch of the room was covered with furniture. Chairs stood on couches that lay on tables; mirrors nearly the height of the door were propped, back to back, against the walls, reflecting and making endless the hills of desks and chairs with their legs in the air, sideboards, dressing tables, chests-of-drawers, more mirrors, empty bookcases, washbasins, clothes cupboards. There was a double bed, carefully made, with the ends of the sheets turned back, lying on top of a dining table on top of another table; there were electric lamps and lampshades, trays and vases, lavatory bowls and basins, heaped in the armchairs that stood on cupboards and tables and beds, touching the ceiling. The one window, looking out on the road, could just be seen through the curved legs of sideboards on their backs. The walls behind the standing mirrors were thick with pictures and picture frames.

Mr. Allingham climbed into the room over a stack of mattresses, then disappeared.

'Hop in, boy.' His voice came up from behind a high kitchen dresser hung with carpets; and, climbing over, Samuel looked down to see him seated on a chair on a couch, leaning back comfortably, his elbow on the shoulder of a statue.

'It's a pity we can't cook here,' Mr. Allingham said. 'There's plenty of stoves, too. That's a meat-safe,' he said, pointing to one corner. 'Just under the bedroom suite.'

'Have you got a piano?'

'There used to be one,' he said. 'I think it's in the other room. She put a carpet over it. Can you play?'

'I can vamp. You can tell what tunes I'm doing, easily. Is the other room like this?'

'Two more rooms, but I think the piano's locked. Yes, there's plenty of furniture,' Mr. Allingham said, looking round with distaste. 'Whenever I say "That's enough now," in she comes with her "Plenty more room, plenty more room." She'll find she can't get in one day, that's what'll happen. Or she can't get out; I don't know which would be the worst. It gets you sometimes you know,' he said, 'all this furniture.'

'Is she your wife, Mr. Allingham?'

'She'll find there's a limit to everything. You get to feel kind of trapped.'

'Do you sleep here?'

'Up there. It's nearly twelve foot high. I've measured. I can touch the ceiling when I wake up.'

'I like this room' Samuel said. 'I think it's perhaps the best room I've ever seen.'

'That's why I brought you. I thought you'd like it. Proper little den for a man with a bottle on his finger, isn't it? I told you, you're not like anybody else. Nobody else can bear the sight of it. Got your cases safe?'

'They're there. In the bath.'

'You keep your eye on them, that's all. I've lost a sofa. One more suite and I'll lose my bed. And what happens when a customer comes? I'll tell you. He takes one peek through the door and off he trots. You can only buy what's on the top at the moment, see.'

'Can you get into the other rooms?'

'You can,' Mr. Allingham said. 'She takes a dive in, head-first. I've lost all interest in the other rooms, myself. You could live and die in there and nobody'd know. There's some nice Chippendale, too. Up by the skylight.'

He rested his other elbow on a hallstand.

'I got to feel lost,' he said. 'That's why I go down to the buffet; there's only tables and chairs there.'

Samuel sat on his perch, swinging the bottle and drumming his feet against the side of a bath mounted yards above the floor of mattresses. A carpet behind him, laid out flat and wide along the air, having no visible support, bore a great earthenware jar dangerously upon the backs of its patterned birds. High over his head, in the tall room, a rocking-chair balanced on a card-table, and the table's thin legs rested on the top of a cupboard standing up straight among pillows and fenders, with its mirrored door wide open.

'Aren't you frightened of things falling? Look at that rocking-chair. One little prod and over she comes.'

'Don't you dare. Of course I'm frightened,' Mr. Allingham said. 'If you open a drawer over there, a wash-stand falls down over here. You've got to be quick as a snake. There's nothing on the top you'd like to buy, is there?'

'I like a lot of the things, but I haven't any money.'

'No, no, you wouldn't have money. That's right. Other people have money.'

'I like the big jar. You could hide a man in that. have you got any soap for my finger?'

'Of course there's no soap, there's only washbasins. You can't have a bath, either, and there's five baths. Why do you want a jar big enough to hide a man in? Nobody I've ever met wants to hide a man in a jar. Everybody else says that jar's too big for anything. Why do you want to find Lucille Harris, Sam?'

'I didn't mean I wanted to hide a man in it. I mean that you could if you wanted to. Oh, a man I know told me about Lucille, Mr. Allingham. I don't know why I want to find her, but that's the only London address I kept. I put the others down the lavatory in the train. When the train was moving.'

'Good, good.' Mr. Allingham put his hand on the thick, white neck of the naked statue, and tightened his fingers.

The door opened on to the landing. Two people came in, and climbed up the mattresses without a word. The first, a fat, short woman with black hair and a Spanish comb, who had painted her face as though it were a wall, took a sudden dive toward the corner behind Samuel and disappeared between two columns of chairs. She must have landed on cushions or a bed, for she made no sound. The second visitor was a tall, youngish man with a fixed smile; his teeth were large, like a horse's, but very white; his glistening fair hair was done in tight curls, and it smelt across the room. He stood on a spring mattress just inside the door, bouncing up and down. 'Come on, Rose, don't be sulky,' he said. 'I know where you've gone.' Then, pretending to see Samuel for the first time, 'Good gracious you look like a bird up there,' he said. 'Is Donald hiding anywhere?'

'I'm not hiding,' Mr. Allingham said. 'I'm by the statue. Sam Bennet, George Ring.'

George Ring bowed and bounced, rising a foot from the mattress.

He and Mr. Allingham could not see each other. Nobody could see the woman with the Spanish comb.

'I hope you've excused the room to Mr. Bennet,' George Ring said. He bounced a few steps in the direction of the hidden statue.

'I don't think it needs any excusing, Mr. Ring,' Samuel said. 'I've never seen such a comfortable room.'

'Oh, but it's terrible.' George Ring was moving up and down rapidly now. 'It's very kind of you to say it's comfortable, but look at the confusion. Just think of living here. You've got something on your finger, did you know that? Three guesses. It's a bottle.' He shook his curls and laughed as he bounced.

'You don't know anything yet,' said Mr. Allingham's voice. The heavy bouncing had shaken down a carpet on to the hallstand and he was hidden as though in another, lower room. 'You don't know anything about him. You wait. What are you bouncing for, George? People don't go bouncing about like a ball as soon as they come into a room.'

'What don't I know about you?' In one leap George Ring was standing directly below Samuel, craning up his curls.

'He doesn't know where he's going, for one thing. And he's looking for a girl he doesn't know called Lucille.'

'Why are you looking for her?' George Ring's head touched the bath. 'Did you see her picture in the paper?'

'No, I don't know anything about her, but I want to see her because she's the only person I know by name in London.'

'Now you know two more, don't you? Are you sure you don't love her?'

'Of course I'm sure.'

'I thought perhaps she might be a sort of Holy Grail. You know what I mean. A sort of ideal.'

'Go on, you big pussycat,' Mr. Allingham said. 'Get me out of here.'

'Is this the first time you've come to London? I felt like that when I came up first, too. Years and years ago. I felt there was something I must find, I can't explain it. Something just round the corner. I searched and searched. I was so innocent. I felt like a sort of knight.'

'Get me out of here,' Mr. Allingham said. 'I feel like the whole room's on top of me.'

'I never found it.' George Ring laughed and sighed and stroked the side of the bath. 'Perhaps you'll be lucky,' he said. 'You'll walk round the corner and there she'll be. Lucille. Lucille. Is she on the telephone?'

'Yes. I've got her number in my book.'

'Oh, that makes it easier, doesn't it. Come on, Rose,' he said. 'I know exactly where you are. She's in a pet.'

Samuel rocked softly on his box in the middle of the furniture.

This was the fullest room in England. How many hundreds of houses had been spilt in here, tables and chairs coming in on a wooden flood, chests and cupboards soaring on ropes through the window and settling down like birds. The other rooms, beyond that jostled door, would be taller and darker even than this, with the mute, black shape of the locked piano mountainous under a shroud of carpets and Rose, with her comb like the prow of a ship, driving into their darkness and lying all night motionless and silent where she struck. Now she was dead still on a sunk bed between the column of chairs, buried alive, soft and fat and lost in a grave in a house.

'I'm going to buy a hammock,' George Ring said. 'I can't bear sleeping under all this furniture.'

Perhaps the room was crowded at night with people who could not see each other, stretched under chairs, under sofas, dizzily asleep on the tops of raised tables, waking up every morning and crying out, 'Earthquake, earthquake!'

'And then I'll go to bed like a sailor.'

'Tell Rose to come and get me out of here,' Mr. Allingham said, behind the cloaked hallstand, 'I want to eat.'

'She's sulking Donald. She's mad about a Japanese screen now.'

'Do you hear that, Sam? Isn't there enough privacy in this room? Anybody can do anything, nobody can see you. I want to eat. I want to have a snack at Dacey's. Are you sleeping here tonight?'

'Who?' Samuel asked. 'Me?'

'You can doss down in one of the other rooms, if you think you can get up again. There's enough beds for a harem.'

'Harem,' George Ring said, pronouncing it another way. 'You've got company, Rose darling. Do come out and be introduced.'

'Thank you, Mr. Allingham,' Samuel said.

'Didn't you really have any idea at all?' George Ring bounced, and for a moment his scented head was level with Samuel's. One wide, bright, horse-toothed smile, and the head was gone. 'About sleeping and things. I think it's awfully brave. You might have fallen in with all kinds of people. "He fell among thieves." Do you know Sir Henry Newbolt's poem?'

'He flung his empty revolver down the slope,' Samuel said.

The day was moving carelessly on to a promised end and in a dark room full of furniture where he'd lie down with his bunch of wives in a crow's-nest bed or rock them in a hammock under the ceiling.

'Goodie goodie! It's so exciting to find someone who knows about poetry. "The voices faded and the hills slept." Isn't that beautiful? The voices faded …? I can read poetry for hours, can't I, Donald? I don't care what kind of poetry it is, I love it all. Do you know, "Is there anybody there, said the traveller?" Where do you put the emphasis, Mr. Bennet? Can I call you Sam? Do you say, "Is there *anybody* there" or "Is there anybody *there*"?'

'It isn't natural,' Mr. Allingham said, 'for a man not to be able to see anybody when he's sitting right next to them. I'm not grumbling, but I can't see anything, that's all. It's like not being in the room.'

'Oh, do be quiet, Donald. Sam and I are having a perfectly serious discussion. Of course you're in the room, don't be morbid.'

'I think I'd put about the same emphasis on all the words,' Samuel said.

'But don't you find it tends to make the line rather flat? "*Is* there anybody there, said the traveller,"' George Ring murmured, pacing the mattresses, his head on one side. 'I feel you do want a stress somewhere.'

Will I be alone tonight in the room with the piano? Samuel wondered. Alone like a man in a warehouse, lying on each bed in turn, opening cupboards and putting my hand in, looking at myself in mirrors in the dark.

'Don't you call me morbid, George Ring,' Mr. Allingham said. He tried to move, but the statue fell against his chair. 'I remember once I drank forty-nine Guinnesses straight off and I came home on the top of a bus. There's nothing morbid about a man who can do that. Right on the top of the bus, too, not just in the upper deck.'

Or will the room be full as a cemetery, but with the invisible dead breathing and snoring all around me, making love in the cupboards, drunk as tailors in the dry baths? Suddenly a warm body might dive in through the door and lie in my bed all night without a name or a word.

'I think forty-nine Guinnesses is piggish,' said George Ring.

'It was raining,' Mr. Allingham said, 'and I never get

truculent. I may sing and I may have a bit of a dance, but I never get nasty. Give me a hand, Sam.'

Samuel took the carpet off the hallstand and pushed the statue away. It had fallen between Mr. Allingham's legs. He came up slowly into sight and rubbed his eyes like a man waking.

'I told you,' he said, 'you get trapped. Coming to Dacey's, George?'

'I'll have to stay for hours, you know that,' George Ring said. 'You know I'm the only person who can humour Rosie when she's in one of her states. Oh, come on, Rosie, don't be temperamental. It's ninety per cent temper and ten per cent mental. Just because you're an actress you think you can stay under the furniture all the afternoon. I'll count five ...'

Samuel followed Mr. Allingham to the door.

'Five, six, seven,' George Ring said, as Mr. Allingham slammed the door hard, and his voice was lost in the noise of furniture falling. They went down the stairs into the hallway that smelt of cabbage, and out on to the grey street.

'I think it must have been the rocking-chair,' Samuel said.

'Mrs. Dacey's is just round the corner,' Mr. Allingham said. 'There you are. See the Cadbury sign?'

2

Mrs. Dacey's front window was whitewashed from inside, and the words 'High Class' had been scrawled across it. '"Susan Dacey, licensed to sell tobacco,"' Samuel read aloud. 'Is it a restaurant too?'

'You must tell her that,' Mr. Allingham said, opening the door. A bell rang. 'It hasn't been called that before.' He held his foot against the door so that the bell kept ringing. 'She's a woman in a thousand.'

A tall, thin, dignified woman came through the private door at the back of the shop, her hands clasped in front of her. She was dressed in black almost down to the ankles, with a severe white collar, and she held her head primly as though it might spill. God help the other nine hundred and ninety-nine. But she smiled then, and her eyes were sharp and light; the dullness raced from her mouth, leaving it cruel and happy.

'Take your trotter off the door,' she said.

The bell stopped.

'That's better. You made enough noise to wake the dead.' She was a well-spoken woman, clear and precise, like a schoolmistress.

'Keeping well, Mrs. Dacey? This is a new friend, Sam Bennet. Two pies and two coffees, please. Where's Polly?'

'Up to no good,' said Mrs. Dacey stepping behind the counter. Her grand dress floated around her. 'You're from the country,' she said, over her shoulder, as she turned the coffee tap on the brass urn. 'How did you find Ikey Mo?'

'That's me.' Mr. Allingham blushed on one side of his face.

'I'm not from the country really.' Samuel told her where he came from. 'I met Mr. Allingham in the station. I'm going to sleep in his flat tonight.'

'I'd sooner sleep in an ashpit,' she said.

The coffee was thick and white and tasteless. They took their cups to a cubicle and Samuel brushed off the crumbs from his chair with his sleeve. His hat was gone. There were small pellets of dirt in the dust at his feet.

'You've got a bottle on your finger,' she said.

'There, you see, everybody notices. Why don't you take it off, Sam? It isn't a decoration, it isn't useful, it's just a bottle.'

'I think my finger must have swollen, Mr. Allingham. The bottle's much tighter now.'

'Let me have a look at you again.' Mrs. Dacey put on a pair of spectacles with steel rims and a hanging chain. 'He's only a baby.'

'I'm twenty.'

'Ikey Mo, the baby farmer.' She walked carefully to the back of the shop and called, 'Polly, come down here. Polly. Polly.'

A girl's voice called back from high up the house, 'What for, ma?'

'Come and get a gentleman's bottle off.'

'It sounds like a Russian composer, doesn't it, darling?' George Ring said, at the door. 'What a marvellous dress, you look like a murderess.'

He sat down next to Samuel.

'I couldn't get Rose to move. She's going to lie there all day in a tantrum. Do tell me what's happening, everybody.'

'It's that bottle again,' Mr. Allingham said. 'Why didn't he put his finger in a glass or something? I don't know what he was poking his finger about for in the first place. It's an enigma to me.'

'Everything's an enigma to you. You can't understand the

slightest touch of originality. I think it must be awful not to have any imagination. It's like a sense of humour.'

'I'm just saying that not to be able to go in and buy a bottle of Bass without having to leave with the bottle on your finger seems to me like a kind of nightmare. That's all I'm saying.'

Samuel heard Mrs. Dacey's daughter running downstairs. Then he saw her hand on the edge of the door. In the second she took to push the door open and come in, he made her a hundred faces; he made her talk and walk in all the disguises of his loves at night; he gave her golden hair, black hair, he knew that she would be gypsy-skinned and white as milk. Polly come and put the kettle on with your white, slender, brown, broad hands, and see me waiting like a grenadier or a caliph in the mousey cubicle.

'It's like one of those nightmares when you're playing billiards and the cue's made of elastic,' Mr. Allingham said.

In came a girl with a long, pale face and glasses. Her hair was not any of Samuel's colours, but only dark and dull.

'Go and help to pull his bottle off,' said Mrs. Dacey.

Polly sat down on the table and took his hand. 'Does it hurt? I've never done it before.' She pulled at his finger.

'I hope you won't ever have to do it again, either,' Mr. Allingham said. 'I don't care if I haven't got any imagination. I'm glad I'm like I am without anything on my finger.'

Polly bent over Samuel's hand and he saw down her dress. She knew that he was looking, but she did not start back or spread her hand across the neck of her dress; she raised her head and stared at his eyes. I shall always remember this, he said to himself. In 1933 a girl was pulling at a bottle on the little finger of my left hand while I looked down her dress. It will last longer than all my poems and troubles.

'I can't get it off,' she said.

'Take him up to the bathroom then and put some soap on it,' said Mrs. Dacey, in her dry, neat voice. 'And mind it's only his bottle.'

George Ring said as they got up to go, 'Scream if you want me, I'll be up in a wink. She's the most terrible person, aren't you, darling? You wouldn't catch little George going up there all alone.'

Polly led the way upstairs.

'I'm not complaining,' Mr. Allingham said, 'I'm just making a statement. I'm not saying it isn't all as it should be. He's got a bottle on his finger and I've got a tooth in my pie.'

His voice faded.

3

Someone had drawn the ragged curtains in the bathroom to shut out the damp old day, and the bath was half full of water with a rubber duck floating on it. As Polly closed and locked the door birds began to sing.

'It's only the birds,' she said. She put the key down her dress. 'You needn't be frightened.'

Two cages hung from the ceiling.

But Samuel had looked frightened when she turned the key and put it away where he never wanted to find it, not when the room grew suddenly like a wood in the tangled shadows of the green curtains.

'It's a funny place to have birds,' he said.

'They're mine.' Polly let the hot water run and the birds sang more loudly as though they heard a waterfall. 'Mr. Allingham comes here for a bath on Wednesdays and he says they sneer at him and blow little raspberries all the time he's washing. But I don't think he washes very much. Doesn't Mr. Allingham make you laugh too?'

He expected her to be smiling when she turned to him, but her face was still and grave, and all at once he saw that she was prettier than any of the girls he had made up in his mind before she opened the door downstairs. He distrusted her prettiness because of the key. He remembered what Mrs. Dacey had said when Mr. Allingham asked where Polly was. 'Up to no good.' He did not think she was going to put her arms around him. That would have been different. If she tried to put his head under the water he'd shout for George Ring and up he'd come like a horse, neighing and smelling of scent.

'I only locked the door because I don't want George Ring to come in. He's queer. He puts scent all over his underclothes; did you know that? The Passing Cloud, that's what we call him. The Passing Cloud.'

'You didn't have to put the key where you put it, though,' Samuel said. 'I might push you down and fish for it, I might be that sort.'

'I don't care.'

If only she would have smiled at him when she said that. But she looked as though she really did not care whether he pushed her down or whether he sat on the edge of the bath and touched the duck with his bottle.

The duck floated in circles on the used, greasy water.

'What's your name?'

'Sam.'

'Mine's Mary. But they call me Polly for short.'

'It isn't much shorter, is it?'

'No, it's exactly the same length.'

She sat by his side on the edge of the bath. He could not think of anything to say. Here was the locked door he had often made up in stories and in his head, in bed in Mortimer Street, and the warm, hidden key, and the girl who was willing for anything. The bathroom should be a bedroom and she should not be wearing glasses.

'Will you take off your glasses, Polly?'

'If you like. But I won't be able to see very far.'

'You don't have to see very far, it's only a little room,' he said. 'Can you see me?'

'Of course I can. You're right next to me. Do you like me better now?'

'You're very pretty, I suppose, Polly.'

'Pretty Polly,' she said, without a smile.

Well, he said to himself, here you are, here she is without any glasses on.

'Nothing ever happens in Sewell Street.' She took his hand and let his finger with the bottle on it lie in her lap.

Her you are, he said, with your hand in her lap.

'Nothing ever happens where I come from, either. I think things must be happening everywhere except where one is. All kinds of things happen to other people. So they say,' he said.

'The man who was lodging next door but one cut his throat like this,' she said, 'before breakfast.'

On his first free days since he was born Samuel sat with a loose girl in a locked bathroom over a tea-shop, the dirty curtains were drawn, and his hand lay on her thighs. He did not feel any emotion at all. O God, he thought, make me feel something, make me feel as I ought to, here is something happening and I'm cool and dull as a man in a bus. Make me remember all the stories. I caught her in my arms, my heart beat against hers, her body was trembling, her mouth opened like a flower. The lotus of Osiris was opening to the sun.

'Listen to the old birds,' she said, and he saw that the hot water was running over the rim of the washbasin.

I must be impotent, he thought.

'Why did he cut his throat like that, Polly? Was it love? I think if I was crossed in love I'd drink brandy and whisky and crème de menthe and that stuff that's made with eggs.'

'It wasn't love with Mr. Shaw. I don't know why he did it. Mrs. Bentley said there was blood everywhere, everywhere, and all over the clock. He left a little note in the letter-rack and all it said was that he'd been meaning to do it ever since October. Look, the water'll drip right through into the kitchen.'

He turned it off. The birds stopped singing.

'Perhaps it was love, really. Perhaps he loved you, Polly, but he wouldn't say so. From a distance.'

'Go on, he had a limp,' she said. 'Old Dot and Carry. How old are you?'

'Twenty.'

'No, you're not.'

'Well, nearly.'

'No you're not.'

Then they were silent, sitting on the bath, his hand in her lap. She trailed her pale hand in the water. The birds began again.

'Pale hands I love,' he said.

'Beside the Shalimar. Do you, Sam? Do you love my hands? That's a funny thing to say.' She looked dully at the long, floating weed in the water and made a wave. 'It's like the evening here.'

'It's like evening in the country,' he said. 'Birds singing and water. We're sitting on a bank by the river now.'

'Having a picnic.'

'And then we're going to take our clothes off and have a swim. Gee, it'll be cold. You'll be able to feel all the fish swimming about.'

'I can hear the 47 bus, too,' she said. 'People are going home to tea. It's cold without any clothes on, isn't it? Feel my arm, it's like snow, only not so white. Pale hands I love,' she began to sing. 'Do you love me altogether?'

'I don't know. I don't think I feel anything like that at all. I never do feel much until afterwards and then it's too late.'

'Now it isn't too late. It isn't too late, Sam. We're alone. Polly and Sam. I'll come and have a swim with you if you like. In the dirty old river with the duck.'

'Don't you ever smile, Polly? I haven't seen you smile once.'

'You've only known me for twenty minutes. I don't like smiling much, I think I look best when I'm serious, like this.' She saddened her eyes and mouth. 'I'm a tragedienne. I'm crying because my lover's dead.'

Slowly tears came to her eyes.

'His name was Sam and he had green eyes and brown hair. He was ever so short. Darling, darling, darling Sam, he's dead.' The tears ran down her cheeks.

'Stop crying now, Polly. Please. Stop crying. You'll hurt yourself.'

But she was crying pitifully.

'Stop it, Polly, pretty Polly.' He put his arm round her shoulders. He kissed her on the cheek. It was warm and wet. 'Nobody's dead, Polly darling,' he said. She cried and moaned his name in the abandon of her made grief, tore at the loose, low neck of her dress, threw back her hair and raised her damp eyes to the birds in their cages and the cracked heavens of the ceiling.

'You're doing it fine,' he said in despair, shaking her shoulders. 'I've never seen such fine crying. Stop now, please, Polly, please, while you can stop.'

Ninety-eight per cent of the human body is water, he thought. Polly Dacey is all salt water. She sat by his side like a flood in an apron.

'I'll do anything you like if you'll only stop,' he said. 'You'll drown yourself, Polly. I'll promise to do anything in the world.'

She dried her eyes on her bare arm.

'I wasn't really breaking my heart, silly. I was only depicting. What'll you do, then? Anything? I can depict being glad because my lover's not really dead, too. The War Office made a mistake.'

'Anything,' he said. 'I want to see you being glad tomorrow. You mustn't do one after the other.'

'It's nothing to me, I can do them all in a row. I can do childbirth and being tight and—'

'You do being quiet. Do being a quiet lady sitting on a bath, Polly.'

'I will if you'll come and have a swim with me. You promised.'
She patted her hair into place.

'Where?'

'In the bath. You get in first, go on. You can't break your
promise.'

George Ring, he whispered, gallop upstairs now and bite your
way through the door. She wants me to sit with my overcoat on
and my bottle on my finger in the cold, greasy bath, in the
half-dark bathroom, under the sneering birds.

'I've got a new suit,' he said.

'Take it off, silly. I don't want you to go in the bath with your
clothes on. Look, I'll put something over the window so you can
undress in the dark. Then I'll undress too. I'll come in the bath
with you. Sam, are you frightened?'

'I don't know. Couldn't we take our clothes off and not go in
the bath? I mean, if we want to take them off at all. Someone might
come in. It's terribly cold, Polly. Terribly cold.'

'You're frightened. You're frightened to lie in the water with
me. You won't be cold for long.'

'But there's no sense in it. I don't want to go in the bath. Let's
sit here and you do being glad, Polly.'

He could not move his hand, she had caught the bottle
between her legs.

'You don't want to be frightened. I'm not any older than you
are,' she said, and her whispering mouth was close to his ear. 'As
soon as you get in the bath I'll jump on top of you in the dark. You
can pretend I'm somebody you love if you don't like me properly.
You can call me any name.' She dug her nails into his hand. 'Give
me your coat, I'll hang it over the window. Dark as midnight,' she
said, as she hung the coat up, and her face in the green light
through the curtains was like a girl's under the sea. Then all the
green went out, and he heard her fumbling. I do not want to
drown. I do not want to drown in Sewell Street off Circe Street, he
whispered under his breath.

'Are you undressing? I can't hear you. Quick, quick, Sam.'

He took off his jacket and pulled his shirt over his head. Take a
good look in the dark, Mortimer Street, have a peek at me in
London.

'I'm cold,' he said.

'I'll make you warm, beautifully warm, Sam.' He could not
tell where she was, but she was moving in the dark and clinking a

glass. 'I'm going to give you some brandy. There's brandy, darling, in the medicine cupboard. I'll give you a big glass. You must drink it right down.'

Naked, he slipped one leg over the edge of the bath and touched the icy water.

Come and have a look at impotent Samuel Bennet from Mortimer Street off Stanley's Grove trembling to death in a cold bath in the dark near Paddington Station. I am lost in the metropolis with a rubber duck and a girl I cannot see pouring brandy into a tooth-glass. The birds are going mad in the dark. It's been such a short day for them, Polly.

'I'm in the bath now.'

'I'm undressing too. Can you hear me?' she said softly. 'That's my dress rustling. Now I'm taking my petticoat off. Now I'm naked.' A cold hand touched him on the face. 'Here's the brandy, Sam. Sam, my dear, drink it up and then I'll climb in with you. I'll love you, Sam, I'll love you up. Drink it all up, then you can touch me.'

He felt the glass in his hand and he lifted it up and drank all that was in it.

'Christ!' he said in a clear, ordinary voice. 'Christ!'

Then the birds flew down and kicked him on the head, carefully between the eyes, brutally on each temple, and he fell back in the bath.

That was all the birds singing under the water, and the sea was full of feathers that swam up his nostrils and into his mouth. A duck as big as a ship sailed up on a drop of water as big as a house and smelt his breath as it spurted out from broken, bleeding lips, like flames and waterspouts. Here came a wave of brandy and birds, and Mr. Allingham, naked as a baby, riding on the top with his birthmark like a rainbow, and George Ring swimming breast-stroke through the open door, and three Mrs. Daceys gliding in yards above the flowing ground.

The darkness drowned in a bright ball of light, and the birds stopped.

4

Voices began to reach him from a great distance, travelling in lavatories in racing trains along a liquid track, diving from the immeasurably high ceiling into the cold sea in the enormous bath.

'Do you see what I see?' That was the voice of the man called Allingham, who slept under the furniture. 'He's taking a little dip.'

'Don't let me look, Donald, he's bare all over.' I know him, Samuel thought. That's George Ring the horse. 'And he's ill too. Silly Sam.'

'Lucky Sam. He's drunk, George. Well, well, well, and he hasn't even got his bottle off. Where's Polly?'

'You look over there,' Mrs. Dacey said. 'Over there on the shelf. He's drunk all the eau de cologne.'

'He must have been thirsty.'

Large, bodiless hands came over the bath and lifted him out.

'He's eccentric,' Mr. Allingham said, as they laid him on the floor, 'that's all I'm saying. I'm not preaching, I'm not condemning. I'm just saying that other people get drunk in the proper places.'

The birds were singing again in the electric dawn as Samuel fell quietly to sleep.

The Followers

It was six o'clock on a winter's evening. Thin, dingy rain spat and drizzled past the lighted street lamps. The pavements shone long and yellow. In squeaking goloshes, with mackintosh collars up and bowlers and trilbies weeping, youngish men from the offices bundled home against the thistly wind—

'Night, Mr Macey.'

'Going my way, Charlie?'

'Ooh, there's a pig of a night!'

'Good night, Mr Swan.'—

and older men, clinging on to the big, black circular birds of their umbrellas, were wafted back, up the gaslit hills, to safe, hot, slippered, weatherproof hearths, and wives called Mother, and old, fond, fleabag dogs, and the wireless babbling.

Young women from the offices, who smelt of scent and powder and wet pixie hoods and hair, scuttled, giggling, arm-in-arm, after the hissing trams, and screeched as they splashed their stockings in the puddles rainbowed with oil between the slippery lines.

In a shop window, two girls undressed the dummies:

'Where you going to-night?'

'Depends on Arthur. Up she comes.'

'Mind her cami-knicks, Edna ...'

The blinds came down over another window.

A newsboy stood in a doorway, calling the news to nobody, very softly:

'Earthquake. Earthquake in Japan.'

Water from a chute dripped on to his sacking. He waited in his own pool of rain.

A flat, long girl drifted, snivelling into her hanky, out of a jeweller's shop, and slowly pulled the steel shutters down with a hooked pole. She looked, in the grey rain, as though she were crying from top to toe.

A silent man and woman, dressed in black, carried the wreaths away from the front of their flower shop into the scented deadly darkness behind the window lights. Then the lights went out.

A man with a balloon tied to his cap pushed a shrouded barrow up a dead end.

A baby with an ancient face sat in its pram outside the wine vaults, quiet, very wet, peering cautiously all round it.

It was the saddest evening I had ever known.

A young man, with his arm round his girl, passed by me, laughing; and she laughed back, right into his handsome, nasty face. That made the evening sadder still.

I met Leslie at the corner of Crimea Street. We were both about the same age: too young and too old. Leslie carried a rolled umbrella, which he never used, though sometimes he pressed doorbells with it. He was trying to grow a moustache. I wore a check, ratting cap at a Saturday angle. We greeted each other formally:

'Good evening, old man.'

'Evening, Leslie.'

'Right on the dot, boy.'

'That's right,' I said. 'Right on the dot.'

A plump, blonde girl, smelling of wet rabbits, self-conscious even in that dirty night, minced past on high-heeled shoes. The heels clicked, the soles squelched.

Leslie whistled after her, low and admiring.

'Business first,' I said.

'Oh, boy!' Leslie said.

'And she's too fat as well.'

'I like them corpulent,' Leslie said. 'Remember Penelope Bogan? a Mrs too.'

'Oh, come *on*. That old bird of Paradise Alley! How's the exchequer, Les?'

'One and a penny. How you fixed?'

'Tanner.'

'What'll it be, then? The Compasses?'

'Free cheese at the Marlborough.'

We walked towards the Marlborough, dodging umbrella spokes, smacked by our windy macs, stained by steaming lamplight, seeing the sodden, blown scourings and street-wash of the town, papers, rags, dregs, rinds, fag-ends, balls of fur, flap, float, and cringe along the gutters, hearing the sneeze and rattle of the bony trams and a ship hoot like a fog-ditched owl in the bay, and Leslie said:

'What'll we do after?'

'We'll follow someone,' I said.

'Remember following that old girl up Kitchener Street? The one who dropped her handbag?'

'You should have given it back.'

'There wasn't anything in it, only a piece of bread-and-jam.'

'Here we are,' I said.

The Marlborough saloon was cold and empty. There were notices on the damp walls: No Singing. No Dancing. No Gambling. No Peddlers.

'You sing,' I said to Leslie, 'and I'll dance, then we'll have a game of nap and I'll peddle my braces.'

The barmaid, with gold hair and two gold teeth in front, like a well-off rabbit's, was blowing on her nails and polishing them on her black marocain. She looked up as we came in, then blew on her nails again and polished them without hope.

'You can tell it isn't Saturday night,' I said. 'Evening, Miss. Two pints.'

'And a pound from the till,' Leslie said.

'Give us your one-and-a-penny, Les,' I whispered and then said aloud: 'Anybody can tell it isn't Saturday night. Nobody sick.'

'Nobody here to *be* sick,' Leslie said.

The peeling, liver-coloured room might never have been drunk in at all. Here, commercials told jokes and had Scotches and sodas with happy, dyed, port-and-lemon women; dejected regulars grew grand and muzzy in the corners, inventing their pasts, being rich, important, and loved; reprobate grannies in dustbin black cackled and nipped; influential nobodies revised the earth; a party, with earrings, called 'Frilly Willy' played the crippled piano, which sounded like a hurdy-gurdy playing under water, until the publican's nosy wife said, 'No.' Strangers came and went, but mostly went. Men from the valleys dropped in for nine or ten; sometimes there were fights; and always there was something doing, some argie-bargie, giggle and bluster, horror or folly, affection, explosion, nonsense, peace, some wild goose flying in the boozy air of that comfortless, humdrum nowhere in the dizzy, ditchwater town at the end of the railway lines. But that evening it was the saddest room I had ever known.

Leslie said, in a low voice: 'Think she'll let us have one on tick?'

'Wait a bit, boy,' I murmured. 'Wait for her to thaw.'

But the barmaid heard me, and looked up. She looked clean through me, back through my small history to the bed I was born in, then shook her gold head.

'I don't know what it is,' said Leslie as we walked up Crimea Street in the rain, 'but I feel kind of depressed to-night.'

'It's the saddest night in the world,' I said.

We stopped, soaked and alone, to look at the stills outside the cinema we called the Itch-pit. Week after week, for years and years, we had sat on the edges of the springless seats there, in the dank but snug, flickering dark, first with toffees and monkey-nuts that crackled for the dumb guns, and then with cigarettes: a cheap special kind that would make a fire-swallower cough up the cinders of his heart. 'Let's go in and see Lon Chaney,' I said, 'and Richard Talmadge and Milton Sills and ... and Noah Beery,' I said, 'and Richard Dix ... and Slim Summerville and Hoot Gibson.'

We both sighed.

'Oh, for our vanished youth,' I said.

We walked on heavily, with wilful feet, splashing the passers-by.

'Why don't you open your brolly?' I said.

'It won't open. You try.'

We both tried, and the umbrella suddenly bellied out, the spokes tore through the soaking cover; the wind danced its tatters; it wrangled above us in the wind like a ruined, mathematical bird. We tried to tug it down: an unseen, new spoke sprang through its ragged ribs. Leslie dragged it behind him, along the pavement, as though he had shot it.

A girl called Dulcie, scurrying to the Itch-pit, sniggered 'Hallo,' and we stopped her.

'A rather terrible thing has happened,' I said to her. She was so silly that, even when she was fifteen, we had told her to eat soap to make her straw hair crinkle, and Les took a piece from the bathroom, and she did.

'I know,' she said, 'you broke your gamp.'

'No, you're wrong there,' Leslie said. 'It isn't *our* umbrella at all. It fell off the roof. *You* feel,' he said. 'You can feel it fell off the roof.' She took the umbrella gingerly by its handle.

'There's someone up there throwing umbrellas down,' I said. 'It may be serious.'

She began to titter, and then grew silent and anxious as Leslie said: 'You never know. It might be walking-sticks next.'

'Or sewing-machines,' I said.

'You wait here, Dulce, and we'll investigate,' Leslie said.

We hurried on down the street, turned a blowing corner and then ran.

Outside Rabiotti's café, Leslie said: 'It isn't fair on Dulcie.' We never mentioned it again.

A wet girl brushed by. Without a word, we followed her. She cantered, long-legged, down Inkerman Street and through Paradise Passage, and we were at her heels.

'I wonder what's the point in following people,' Leslie said, 'it's kind of daft. It never gets you anywhere. All you do is follow them home and then try to look through the window and see what they're doing and mostly there's curtains anyway. I bet nobody else does things like that.'

'You never know,' I said. The girl turned into St Augustus Crescent, which was a wide lamplit mist. 'People are always following people. What shall we call her?'

'Hermione Weatherby,' Leslie said. He was never wrong about names. Hermione was fey and stringy, and walked like a long gym-mistress, full of love, through the stinging rain.

'You never know. You never know what you'll find out. Perhaps she lives in a huge house with all her sisters—'

'How many?'

'Seven. All full of love. And when she gets home they all change into kimonos and lie on divans with music and whisper to each other and all they're doing is waiting for somebody like us to walk in, lost, and then they'll all chatter round us like starlings and put us in kimonos too, and we'll never leave the house until we die. Perhaps it's so beautiful and soft and noisy—like a warm bath full of birds ...'

'I don't want birds in my bath,' said Leslie. 'Perhaps she'll slit her throat if they don't draw the blinds. I don't care what happens so long as it's interesting.'

She slip-slopped round a corner into an avenue where the neat trees were sighing and the cosy windows shone.

'I don't want old feathers in the tub,' Leslie said.

Hermione turned in at number thirteen, Beach-view.

'You can see the beach all right,' Leslie said, 'if you got a periscope.'

We waited on the pavement opposite, under a bubbling lamp, as Hermione opened her door, and then we tiptoed across and down the gravel path and were at the back of the house, outside an uncurtained window.

Hermione's mother, a round, friendly, owlish woman in a pinafore, was shaking a chip-pan on the kitchen stove.

'I'm hungry,' I said.

'Ssh!'

We edged to the side of the window as Hermione came into the kitchen. She was old, nearly thirty, with a mouse-brown shingle and big earnest eyes. She wore horn-rimmed spectacles and a sensible, tweed costume, and a white shirt with a trim bow-tie. She looked as though she tried to look like a secretary in domestic films, who had only to remove her spectacles and have her hair cherished, and be dressed like a silk dog's dinner, to turn into a dazzler and make her employer Warner Baxter, gasp, woo, and marry her; but if Hermione took off her glasses, she wouldn't be able to tell if he was Warner Baxter or the man who read the meters.

We stood so near the window, we could hear the chips spitting.

'Have a nice day in the office, dear? There's weather,' Hermione's mother said, worrying the chip-pan.

'What's *her* name, Les?'

'Hetty.'

Everything there in the warm kitchen, from the tea-caddy and the grandmother clock, to the tabby that purred like a kettle, was good, dull, and sufficient.

'Mr Truscott was something awful,' Hermione said as she put on her slippers.

'Where's her kimóno?' Leslie said.

'Here's a nice cup of tea,' said Hetty.

'Everything's nice in that old hole,' said Leslie, grumbling. 'Where's the seven sisters like starlings?'

It began to rain much more heavily. It bucketed down on the black back yard, and the little comfy kennel of a house, and us, and the hidden, hushed town, where, even now, in the haven of the Marlborough, the submarine piano would be tinning 'Daisy,' and the happy henna'd women squealing into their port.

Hetty and Hermione had their supper. Two drowned boys watched them enviously.

'Put a drop of Worcester on the chips,' Leslie whispered; and by God she did.

'Doesn't anything happen anywhere?' I said, 'in the whole wide world? I think the *News of the World* is all made up. Nobody murders no one. There isn't any sin any more, or love, or death, or pearls and divorces and mink-coats or anything, or putting arsenic in the cocoa ...'

'Why don't they put on some music for us,' Leslie said, 'and do a dance? It isn't every night they got two fellows watching them in the rain. Not *every* night, anyway!'

All over the dripping town, small lost people with nowhere to go and nothing to spend were gooseberrying in the rain outside wet windows, but nothing happened.

'I'm getting pneumonia,' Leslie said.

The cat and the fire were purring, grandmother time tick-tocked our lives away. The supper was cleared, and Hetty and Hermione, who had not spoken for many minutes, they were so confident and close in their little lighted box, looked at one another and slowly smiled.

They stood still in the decent, purring kitchen, facing one another.

'There's something funny going to happen,' I whispered very softly.

'It's going to begin,' Leslie said.

We did not notice the sour, racing rain any more.

The smiles stayed on the faces of the two still, silent women.

'It's going to begin.'

And we heard Hetty say in a small secret voice: 'Bring out the album, dear.'

Hermione opened a cupboard and brought out a big, stiff-coloured photograph album, and put it in the middle of the table. Then she and Hetty sat down at the table, side by side, and Hermione opened the album.

'That's Uncle Eliot who died in Porthcawl, the one who had the cramp,' said Hetty.

They looked with affection at Uncle Eliot, but we could not see him.

'That's Martha-the-woolshop, you wouldn't remember her, dear, it was wool, wool, wool, with her all the time; she wanted to be buried in her jumper, the mauve one, but her husband put his foot down. He'd been in India. That's your Uncle Morgan,' Hetty said, 'one of the Kidwelly Morgans, remember him in the snow?'

Hermione turned a page. 'And that's Myfanwy, she got queer all of a sudden, remember. It was when she was milking. That's your cousin Jim, the Minister, until they found out. And that's our Beryl,' Hetty said.

But she spoke all the time like somebody repeating a lesson: a well-loved lesson she knew by heart.

We knew that she and Hermione were only waiting.

Then Hermione turned another page. And we knew, by their secret smiles, that this was what they had been waiting for.

'My sister Katinka,' Hetty said.

'Auntie Katinka,' Hermione said. They bent over the photograph.

'Remember that day in Aberystwyth, Katinka?' Hetty said softly. 'The day we went on the choir outing.'

'I wore my new white dress,' a new voice said.

Leslie clutched at my hand.

'And a straw hat with birds,' said the clear, new voice.

Hermione and Hetty were not moving their lips.

'I was always a one for birds on my hat. Just the plumes of course. It was August the third, and I was twenty-three.'

'Twenty-three come October, Katinka,' Hetty said.

'That's right, love,' the voice said. 'Scorpio I was. And we met Douglas Pugh on the Prom and he said: "You look like a queen to-day, Katinka," he said, "You look like a queen, Katinka," he said. Why are those two boys looking in at the window?'

We ran up the gravel drive, and around the corner of the house, and into the avenue and out on to St Augustus Crescent. The rain roared down to drown the town. There we stopped for breath. We did not speak or look at each other. Then we walked on through the rain. At Victoria corner, we stopped again.

'Good night, old man,' Leslie said.

'Good night,' I said.

And we went our different ways.